SECOND CHANCE ON THE CORNER OF MAIN STREET

SECOND *Chance* ON THE CORNER OF *Main*

A *Nestled Hollow* ROMANCE

MEG EASTON

Book One in the Nestled Hollow Romance series

Copyright © 2018 by Meg Easton

ISBN 10: 1723911879

ISBN 13: 978-1723911873

ASIN: B07HKR7PHZ

Cover Illustration by Blue Water Books

Interior Design by Mountain Heights Publishing

Author website: www.megeaston.com

For my husband, Lance

Chapter One

*W*hitney sat at her desk in the Nestled Hollow Gazette, moving each of the day's articles into their place in the layout. She glanced up at one of the other occupied desks in this three-desk office. "Scott, how is the business spotlight coming?"

"Still working on it," Scott said, not taking his eyes off his computer screen.

"Kara, how close are you on the repaving article?"

"I need three minutes."

The door burst open, and a red-faced third grader ran in, clutching a paper in his hand.

Whitney stood up. "Lincoln— did you run all the way here from school?"

Lincoln bent over, his hands on his knees, panting. Between heaving breaths, he said, "Yep. I had to stay after to finish my math, so I ran to get here at the normal time."

"You don't have to hurry over here so quickly," Whitney said, grabbing a water bottle from their mini fridge and handing it to him. "It's okay if you come later, or even if you have to miss a day."

He handed a paper to Whitney and opened the water bottle, taking a few gulps. "Nope, a junior reporter always meets his deadlines." And then he saluted her, and she saluted him right back.

As Whitney turned, Lincoln grabbed her arm. "Wait. I didn't see what your shirt said today, and it's a new one, right?" Whitney turned back around as Lincoln read it out loud and laughed. "'I'm a superhero dressed as a reporter.' That one's my new favorite."

Whitney grinned. At the beginning of the school year, Lincoln had stopped in every single day for a week, begging to be a "junior reporter" and bring her the articles he wrote during recess at school. She hadn't wanted to squash the dreams of someone so passionate about journalism, so she'd told him yes. She could tell that he tried so hard on his handwriting that she decided to scan his article and print it exactly as he wrote it instead of typing it out like a normal article, and his feature was an instant hit. It had prompted her to talk to the teacher of the journalism class at the middle school, and they started a "journalist for the day" program in their class. Whitney would've killed for the opportunity to have a by-line in elementary school or middle school.

Just as Lincoln was walking out the door, he held it open for Evia, an older woman with extra fluffy hair, as she stepped inside. "Hello, Whitney. I'm just stopping in on my way to market and wanted to tell you that apparently that storm last night blew a giant branch clean off the Amherst's tree. And you know they're both too old to be cleaning up a mess like that. But on my way, I saw a den of Cub Scouts gathering to haul off the mess. I snapped a picture with my phone," she held it out as evidence, "but I don't know how to get the picture off this blasted thing and over to you."

Whitney helped her to email the picture to Whitney's email account and thanked Evia for the story. As Evia was walking out the door, Whitney smiled. She had lived in this town for her entire life, so they'd seen every awkward phase she'd gone through and every mistake she'd made. And she'd had some incredibly awkward phases and made some pretty big mistakes. She didn't pause nearly often enough to think about how far she'd come, and how great it was to have a town who trusted her. When Mr. Annesley had retired and left the newspaper to her, and then died in a car crash that same weekend three years ago, Whitney would've never guessed that so many people would stop in and give her every story idea they had. She was actually successful at publishing a small town newspaper, when most print newspapers in the country were a thing of the past. The Nestled Hollow Gazette succeeded because it kept its focus on showcasing all the people in the town.

Kara clicked her mouse with a flourish of her hand and called out, "Sent!"

At sixteen years old, Kara was the same age now that Whitney was when she first started working at the Gazette. They both made their way to Whitney's desk and Whitney switched over to her email and opened the file. She read as Kara hovered. The article told about all the potholes on Silver Mine Street, and how unsightly it was and how difficult to drive on, and how beautiful it was going to look when finished.

Whitney looked up at the girl and remembered how eager she had been to please Mr. Annesley when she was first learning the business. She hoped when she was training her young staff that she had the same determination to get it right

3

while still showing a kind sparkle in her eye, just like Mr. Annesley'd had.

"What's the lead on this?"

"Fixing the road," Kara said, like it was the only possible answer. Then her brow crinkled and she paused for a moment before Whitney saw her eyes travel up to the big vinyl letters on the wall behind Whitney's desk— *The lead is the people.* "Wait, it's not the road. But how do I make the people the lead on this?"

Whitney lifted one shoulder. "Who does the damaged road affect? Who will construction affect?"

Kara's eyes looked off into the distance, not really focusing on anything. "Elsmore Market is right on that corner. It won't really affect their customers, but they get access to their employee lot from Silver Mine. Mrs. Davenport lives on Silver Mine, and she has a hard enough time pulling out of her driveway onto a regular road. She might need some help. Oh! And there's a whole neighborhood of kids who ride their bikes down that street to get to the elementary school." With each person she mentioned, Kara's smile grew wider, and Whitney's grew wider right along with it. "I've got a lot of people I need to talk to. Can I get you this article after your Main Street Business Alliance meeting?" Kara glanced at the clock on the wall. "Hey, shouldn't you have already left for that?"

Whitney looked up at the clock that read 3:55, and made a sound like a choked hyena. She smoothed down the front of her t-shirt and dark jeans and grabbed her black blazer off the back of her chair, pushing her arms into the sleeves as she walked to the door. "I've got to run."

"My article will be in your email when you get back," Scott called out as she waved and walked out the door.

She rushed down the street to the old library, followed the

sidewalk around to the back of the building, and went down the cement stairs to the basement door and hurried inside.

Yes! There was still a seat on the front row. Whitney sat down next to her friend Brooke. There was a time not that long ago where Whitney would've felt pangs of inadequacy sitting next to someone as fashionable and put together as Brooke, but apparently Whitney had come a long way on that front, too. She liked the outfit she'd adopted as her uniform when she became the owner and editor-in-chief of the paper. It honored the old newspaper pun t-shirt and jeans-wearing version of herself, yet gave the impression that maybe she had a clue what she was doing when she'd swapped out the stylish jeans of her teenage years for the darker, nicer looking ones and added the blazer.

"I've got a headline for tomorrow morning's paper," Brooke said. "*The World Ended at,*" she glanced down at her watch, "*three fifty-eight on Thursday.*"

Whitney laughed and then rolled her eyes. "Just because you beat me here for the first time in history doesn't mean—"

Brooke held up a finger. "I beat you here for the first time in history *and* you were very nearly late. I'm pretty sure both are signs of the apocalypse."

Tory, a woman sitting in the row behind them who lived in a house next to Whitney's apartment building, leaned forward. "I've got some leads on an article for you. Are you going to be home tonight?"

"Not if I can help it."

The woman chuckled. "Yeah, you're definitely a busy one. Should I just bring it by the newspaper then?"

Whitney nodded. "I'll be there until probably eight."

Whitney turned back to face the front, and Brooke folded her arms, giving Whitney a knowing look. "What?"

Brooke raised an eyebrow. "You know, normal people aren't gone this much. Normal people actually *like* to go home at the end of the day, relax a bit after working so hard."

"My house isn't relaxing; it's *boring*."

"Because there's no one there, and you're addicted to being around people?"

There were very few people other than Brooke who could pull off a question like that and not sound rude. But it still stung. Whitney just shrugged and didn't answer.

"When was the last time you went on a date?"

"You know I don't date."

"I know I care about my friend who loves people, and want her to be able to go home at night and not be alone. And the only way that's going to happen, my friend, is if you date."

"I don't need to go on a date to not be alone." She spread her arms wide. "I've got this entire town to keep me company." When Brooke opened her mouth to say something more, Whitney added "Shush. The meeting's about to start."

Chapter Two

$\mathcal{E}$li shielded his eyes as the mid-morning sun shone down on all twenty-two people at the TeamUp training grounds. He switched his headset mic to *on*. "It looks like teams one and three have managed to get their ropes through the bucket handle without touching the bucket. A hearty high five to you both!"

"And now team three has their rope through their bucket handle," Eli's business partner, Ben, said from the other side of the playing field.

Eli chuckled as team four still strategized in a huddle, arms interlocked, heads down in the middle, looking more like a rugby scrum than five tech development and sales team members. "Team four— how you doing over there?"

One head poked up, and he freed an arm long enough to give him a thumbs up.

The three other teams each had a team member at either end of their rope, the bucket swaying in the middle, carrying their bucket of water, or "toxic waste," to the waste site.

When Eli and Ben made their way to each other, watching

the teams' progress, Ben switched off his mic and said, "Shouldn't you have already taken off?"

Eli glanced over at the open grassy space where they'd set up all the inflatable obstacles for arrow tag— the next challenge, and his favorite one to facilitate. Maybe if he just planned to drive late into the night, he could stay here until late afternoon.

"Avert your eyes," Ben said. "You know you can't stay for that." He switched back on his mic. "Whoa! Team four has left their huddle in a burst of energy. Look at that speed! They're catching up!"

Eli and Ben both moved to the edge of the playing field, where four "waste reclamation facilities" stood, each with a six foot wide circle painted on the ground, and in the center of each circle sat an empty bucket on top of a stool. All four teams reached their circles at nearly the same time, their buckets hanging from the middle of the rope strung between at least two players.

"Remember," Eli said, "that circle represents the radiation zone, and that zone goes all the way up to the sky. Don't let any part of your body cross over into the radiation zone, or you lose it."

"Your dad's going in for surgery tomorrow morning, right?" Ben said, covering his mic. "Nestled Hollow is in the center of Colorado so that's like, what, a fifteen-hour drive?"

Eli shook his head and covered his mic. "More like eighteen or nineteen." He adjusted his mic and said, "Teams, have you figured out how to use that second rope to help dump that bucket, since you can't go inside the circle or touch it? Time to get that rope out!"

"So I guess you won't be there before your dad goes into surgery, then," Ben said. "Watch your hands! Don't let it go over the edge of the circle! When do you have to report in at the family business?"

"I have to be in town for a meeting at four o'clock. Cindy, you reached over the circle with that last adjustment! You just lost that hand— you'll have to keep it behind your back from here on out. Team three, she's struggling to keep that bucket from tipping— help her out!"

Eli watched in silence as all teams stood with two members each standing on opposite sides of their circles, the rope stretched between them, the bucket hovering in the middle, near the bucket they needed to dump it into. Two more players from each team were stretching the second rope out between them, and each moving into place.

It was amazing how well StylesTech had improved since the beginning of the week. StylesTech management had sent two departments to TeamUp— sales and development, because they couldn't stop arguing and blaming each other. Eli and Ben had mixed up the teams for each challenge and only two and a half days later, both teams were working together like pros.

Man, he loved his job. It was ridiculous how much he was going to miss it while he was gone.

All four teams guided the second rope to push against the bottom portion of the bucket, while the two team members with the rope through the handle were pulling forward, causing their buckets to tip, pouring the water into the empty bucket on the stool.

"And team four has finished!" Eli called out, while team four celebrated.

"And team two!" Ben said. "Oh! Bad news, two, Frank just cheered a little too close to the radiation and just lost an arm and a leg. Bummer, Frank. Looks like you'll be hopping for a while."

"Team three finished!"

"And team one!"

Eli made a show of putting on an invisible radiation suit, complete with helmet, and went inside each circle to see which teams had managed to get enough of their toxic waste into the reclamation facility.

He stepped out of the last circle, pretended to take off the radiation suit and announced, "All four teams completed the challenge. TeamUp—"

All twenty StylesTech employees shot a fist into the air and yelled, "To triumph!"

Eli glanced over at the dirt parking lot at the edge of the training fields, where his car sat packed with everything he'd need to stay in Nestled Hollow for the next four to six weeks, and sighed.

Ben clapped his hands together. "We've got cold water and Gatorades and fruits and other snacks for you before we head into arrow tag. But first, we've got one more team activity."

Eli's attention shifted to Ben. This wasn't in the schedule. Ben didn't look at him, though; he just kept his eyes on the twenty team members of StylesTech.

"You all know that Eli here isn't going to be here for the rest of the week, because he's got to head to Colorado. You're all so much fun, though, that Eli doesn't want to leave. What do you think, StylesTech? Can you TeamUp to get him to his car?"

Eli laughed a big hearty laugh as they swarmed him, lifted him up in the air, and carried him to his car, setting him down by his car door.

"Well, that was a first." Eli laughed again. "You all really are rock stars. Remember that first challenge where you were supposed to lead the blindfolded person through the mine field of plastic cups filled with water, but instead you led the blindfolded to step right on every one? And now, not even midday on Wednesday, and you all pretty much just saved the world from an apocalypse with that Toxic Waste challenge. I think I got a little dust in my eye." He wiped his eye like he was wiping away a tear, and everyone laughed.

Ben motioned like he was pushing them all away. "Now get on over to the snack table and hydrate, everyone!"

Eli glanced at Ben and then shook his head, smiling, as he turned off his mic and removed his headset, handing it to Ben.

Ben took off his, too. "You know I've got your back. Or, I guess I'm good at instructing other people to have your back. Now stop worrying about heading home. It can't be that bad. And hey— maybe you'll even meet a girl while you're there."

Eli thought of the one girl he'd ever fallen in love with and the look on her face when he'd driven away from Nestled Hollow twelve years ago. "Ha. Not likely."

"Oh, come on," Ben said, laughing. "You'll be there a month and a half. Maybe you can up your longest relationship record from two weeks to, I don't know, maybe even three." He paused a moment, then in a more serious voice, said, "Going home is always hard. Especially when you haven't been there in twelve years."

Eli glanced west— the direction of home— and took a deep breath. "Yes it is. Especially when you and your business partner were ready to implement a plan to grow the business."

"Don't worry," Ben said, clapping him on the back. "I'll hold down the fort while you're gone. Once you're back, we'll put the plan into play as if you'd never left."

In an effort to drown out any thoughts about where he was headed and what might happen when he got there, Eli blasted music from the moment he got on the freeway in Sacramento until late that night when he stopped at a hotel in downtown Salt Lake City. He was on the road again before eight in the morning, and the music did a good job of drowning his thoughts for the first six hours. But the closer he got to his childhood home, and the more he got texts from his mom saying that his dad's ankle surgery had gone well and that he was recovering in the hospital, the more his mind went to the town that didn't love him, the dad he could never please, and the girl he'd left behind all those years ago.

The road wound between two mountains, and as soon as he came around the last bend, Nestled Hollow came into view, in a small valley with the freeway on one side and mountains forming the other three sides, the lake sparkling in the sunlight at one end, and his childhood came rushing back at him. This view had been forever burned into his memory, but seeing it again in person— as a thirty-year-old now— was different. He exited the freeway and made his way through town, memories hitting him one after another at a rapid pace, flooding his mind with every turn.

He turned on to Main Street, with its creek running right down the middle of the street, separating one side of the road from the other, and drove past Treanor Outdoor Rentals, the family business that was his to run for the next four to six weeks. The place brought back surprisingly happy memories — as a kid he had dreamed of one day growing up and running the family business. He'd loved Treanor's. There was no way he'd choose to run it now, unless his dad wasn't in the picture.

He drove to the end of the second block, just past the clock tower that straddled Snowdrift Springs, did a U-turn at the bridge covering the creek, then found a parking spot right near the library. As soon as he opened his door, he took a deep breath of the crisp mountain air that carried with it the faint scent of pine trees and fresh lakes and good, fertile dirt. As much as he didn't want to be here, he had sure missed that scent.

Eli glanced down at his watch as he walked toward the back of the building— 4:09. Perfect. He figured if he stepped in after the meeting started, it would minimize having to talk to everyone before he was ready. He walked into the downstairs meeting hall. About twenty-five people filled the space, and although there were a few empty seats still, every seat in the back row had been taken. Instead of interrupting the meeting by squeezing in somewhere in the middle, he leaned against the wall at the back.

Eli's dad had brought him to these meetings every week from about age ten until age seventeen, when Eli's parents separated and he started rebelling against everything his dad wanted him to do. He smiled to see that, even after all these years, Ed and Linda Keetch were still running the Main Street Business Alliance. She was talking about the plans for Fall Market, and which Main Street businesses were helping out with what.

And that's when he saw Whitney sitting in the front row and his breath caught in his throat. Every time he'd thought of her over the past twelve years— and he was embarrassed to admit how frequently that was— he had always pictured her still here in town. But he hadn't dared to hope that she was actually still here.

Her hair was shorter— it brushed her shoulders now, but still had big curls and was the same rich auburn color he'd recognize anywhere. He hadn't seen her in twelve years, yet being in the same room with her still caused a fire to burn in his chest and made him no longer able to think straight. Maybe, hopefully, she would turn enough that he could get a glimpse of her face.

Linda glanced down at her clipboard. "I've already made a few assignments— the plans that Joey's Pizza and Subs and Paws and Relax have to bring in tourists really seem to be coming together so nicely. Let's move on to the decorations for Main Street," she said. "The snow pack for this winter is predicted to be the lowest we've seen in a couple of decades, so things are going to get tight for all of us when it comes to the bottom line. We need this Fall Market to be better attended than ever before to make up the difference in revenue we can expect at each of our businesses this winter. So things are going to need to be truly spectacular this year. Next in line for their turn at decorations are the Nestled Hollow Gazette and Treanor's Outdoor Rentals."

Eli stood up straight, feeling like he'd just been hit by an explosion. He hadn't even been in town five minutes, and already he was getting assigned to be on a committee. And heaven help him if Whitney was here with the Gazette. That's where she'd worked back in high school, but hopefully she'd changed professions. He couldn't be teamed up with her, not after being gone for so long. He wondered if she was still angry about the way he'd left all those years ago.

Whitney's hand shot into the air. "Maybe we should switch

that assignment to someone other than Treanor's. Robert will be out of commission until well after Fall Market."

"It'll be just fine, dear." Linda met Eli's eyes and gave a nod. "Robert's son is here to run the store in his absence. He can partner with you for the decorations."

Whitney whipped around in her seat, confusion on her face, until her eyes met Eli's. Then her expression changed.

Yep. She was still angry.

Chapter Three

*N*o. Eli could not be here. Not after all this time.

"Who's the hottie?" Brooke asked as Ed Keetch talked about something Whitney couldn't focus on.

She turned back to face the front, crossing her arms. She couldn't believe that Linda Keetch paired Eli with her. Surely she knew better. She could've fudged the schedule a bit so that Treanor's would help out with Thanksgiving instead. Eli would've never known.

Brooke let out a little gasp. "You *know* the hottie."

Whitney snuck one more glance back at him and met Eli's eyes. Apparently he hadn't stopped looking at her, either. She huffed as she turned her attention back to Ed Keetch.

"And not only do you know him," Brooke said, her eyes searching Whitney, "but you *dated* him."

"Stop using your acute powers of observation on me."

The moment Linda Keetch ended the meeting, Whitney bolted up to her. "Linda, I don't know if you knew how things ended with Eli and me—"

Linda Keetch smiled and interrupted, saying, "Sweetie, *everyone* knew."

"Then why pair us together for the decorations? This is the fortieth anniversary of the Fall Market. Surely you want people who can actually work together to decorate." From the corner of her eye, Whitney saw Eli approaching, coming within hearing distance. She glanced his direction without letting her eyes fall directly on him, then turned back to Linda Keetch. "I'm sure he just got into town, and probably isn't staying long."

"Just pulled into town moments ago," Eli said, obviously having overheard. "And I'll be staying four to six weeks to run Treanor's. Nice to see you, Whitney. You look amazing."

His voice came out low and deeper than she remembered. The last part had been quieter, like he only meant for her to hear it, and her cheeks flushed despite her express wishes that they wouldn't.

"See?" Whitney said, holding both hands out to Eli, presenting the evidence of exactly why this wouldn't work. "He just got into town. And he'll be running a business he's never run before. He'll need to spend his time getting his feet under him, not planning Main Street Fall Market decorations."

"All true. Plus, I haven't even seen what Main Street Fall Market decorations look like for the past dozen years."

Good. He was trying to get out of this, too.

Linda Keetch smiled as she placed one wrinkled hand lightly on each of their forearms. "We need you both. It'll all work out, I promise. You two will do great work together." Then she turned, looped her arm in Ed Keetch's, and they exited the room.

Whitney forced a smile on her face and turned to Eli. "Well, I guess we'll be working together." She had thought of him so many times over the past twelve years. She hadn't realized that, all along, she'd been picturing him as the eighteen-year-old version of himself. This thirty-year-old man caught her off guard. Things would be so much easier if that extra twelve years hadn't looked so good on him.

"Maybe we can get out of it somehow."

Whitney looked at Ed's and Linda's retreating figures. "I'm sure you remember Ed and Linda. It's not going to happen."

Eli grimaced. "Yeah. I'm not even sure that a death certificate from the coroner would be enough to get out of this."

"Do you remember old man Roberts? He promised the Keetch's that he'd provide bales of hay for the hay ride one year, but he died before he actually provided them. They still mysteriously showed up, though, so I think you may be on to something."

"I don't know about you, but when I die, I want to be in heaven thinking about nothing but rest and recreation, not planning the Fall Market decorations." Eli held up a hand, pinky finger outstretched, and said, "I promise not to die before finishing these decorations."

Whitney looked at his pinky, poised for her to reach out with her pinky and intertwine it with his, waiting for her to promise the same to him. She kept her arms at her sides. The banter had definitely eased a very awkward moment, but underneath, things were still awkward. And so much had changed over the years; she couldn't just go back to acting like none of it had happened.

It wasn't that she didn't have anything to say to him. There had been so many things she'd wanted to say to him over the years. Things she wanted him to say to her. But not here. Not with an audience.

In fact, maybe not ever. She had been doing just fine

without Eli Treanor in her life. Hearing his explanations now would only cause her pain. So would continuing to talk like they were just random acquaintances. There was much too big of a damaged part of her heart with his name on it to just pretend.

"It's good to see you again, Eli," she said, working to keep her voice even amidst the swirl of emotions working inside her. "Now if you'll excuse me, I have to go."

"Wait," Eli said as she walked out the door. She didn't wait, though; she just kept walking. As she rounded the side of the building, he jogged around her and stopped right in front of her, causing her to stop, too. "It's been a long time. Can we talk?"

"No."

Whitney moved to walk around him, but he held up a hand. "Please?"

She let out a deep breath and crossed her arms. What she most needed was some time to adjust to the news that he was back after all this time, not be thrown into talking to him. She opened her mouth to talk, and years' worth of frustration came spilling out. "You're right. It *has* been a long time. You were my best friend, Eli, all through high school. My boyfriend for four months. We talked multiple times a day and told each other everything. I can't tell you how many times I've wanted to talk since you left. But twelve years is a long time. I think we're past that point."

Eli dropped his arm. "I shouldn't have come back."

"No," Whitney said, unsure of what she even wanted from him. "Of course you should've come back. I just..." She stopped, not knowing how she wanted to end the sentence. She just wished he'd never come back? That she would've known he was coming? That things had been different?

"I should've called first."

"So many times."

He flinched, like her words stung him. But then he pulled out his phone, apparently more interested in it than the conversation that he had instigated. His brow crinkled, and then he slid his phone back into his pocket and said, "You're right. I'm sorry—I've got to go."

He didn't wait around for her response, so she called out to him, "When are we going to meet about the decorations?"

"I'll text you," he called back as he jogged to his car, not even turning fully to meet her eyes.

Whitney hadn't even noticed that Brooke had made her way outside until she stepped next to her and said, "If he looks this good in slacks and a button down, can you even imagine him in a suit?"

They both stared at his car as he drove away. So many emotions battled for dominance in Whitney right now that she couldn't have named a single one. Except maybe confusion. Or bewilderment. Once upon a time, she used to look for him everywhere, and sadness had hit her hard whenever she'd hoped to see him and didn't. It had been so long, though, since she'd last looked for him that seeing him in town caught her completely off guard.

"Please tell me that you're going to suspend your 'no dating' rule while he's here. Please."

"Did you not see how that just went? The angry words and him blowing me off?"

Brooke shrugged. "Angry words, sure. But from where I stood, all I could see was sparks flying."

Whitney rolled her eyes.

"He said he'd text you," Brooke said, like it was evidence of sparks.

"He doesn't even have my number," Whitney said as she took the last few steps to the front sidewalk.

"Are you heading back to the paper?"

Whitney shook her head. "Kara is still out working on her story, and won't be back until seven. Scott emailed me his articles during the meeting and then headed out, so no one's there. I think I'm just going to go work on some interviews I need for a couple of stories."

"So what I'm hearing is that you're free tonight, and there's someone new in town who could use someone showing him the changes around town."

"Brooke. I'm not interested in dating Eli, or taking him around town, or doing anything with him outside of the decorations that we have to do. The last time I had a relationship with Eli, he left, throwing all our plans to the wind, and it took two years to get over him. Just because his parents made him come back, and he came back looking good doesn't change the fact that I've been mad at him for the past twelve years. And it doesn't change the fact that *I don't date*." She emphasized each word, hoping that Brooke would know she was serious.

After a small pause, she added, "Aren't you flying away somewhere soon? You've spent a record three weeks in Nestled Hollow. I had it on good authority that staying so long in one location could make you shrivel up into a little lump of Brooke on the road."

"I made some new dress designs, and I had to make sure my team was set and ready to go into production before I could leave. There's a great party in L.A. in two days, though, where I might get a one-on-one with fashion mogul Izic Vega himself. And I have never met anyone who is as expert as you are at surrounding herself with people while simultaneously pushing them away."

"That's why you're the perfect best friend. You never stay in one place long enough to be pushed away."

"Unless I stay for three weeks, apparently." Brooke laughed and bumped her shoulder into Whitney's, knocking her off the edge of the sidewalk and onto the road. Whitney laughed and gave Brooke a playful two-armed push. Brooke laughed along with her, and wound her arm with Whitney's. "Well, I'm going back to the store. You go ahead and get to surrounding yourself with all the people who aren't that hot man who's interested in you."

"Based on the past twelve years, I'm pretty sure it's safe to say he's not interested. But don't you ever let someone tell you that you're not an optimist."

"I wear that badge with honor," Brooke said as she twisted away from Whitney's arm, did an exaggerated bow, and then danced off into her shop.

Whitney pulled out her notebook and flipped through the pages until she got to her list of articles that weren't time sensitive that she wanted to do for either the *Business Spotlight* feature, or the *Our Town, Our People* feature. She ran her finger down the list and stopped at Paws and Relax, one of the Main Street businesses that had only been around for a couple of years but was a big hit. If she hadn't been so distracted after the meeting, she'd have grabbed Macie, the owner, and asked for an interview then. She caught Macie at her store, though, and interviewed her as she managed a mom and tot play group with a bunch of puppies in the mix, and got some great candid shots for the article. When they were finished, Whitney went outside to get some shots of the building itself. But now that she'd had time to calm down from their surprise meeting and let his being back in town sink in a bit, she found herself spending more time sneaking peeks toward the business at the other end of Main Street— Treanor's Outdoor Rentals.

She wondered for the billionth time what Eli had been up to since he left. In college, she'd taken an investigative journalism class, and had used everything she'd learned to search for him. But it was like he'd fallen off the planet. Years later, she'd found the website for his company, TeamUp, and found his Instagram account, but it only contained pictures from TeamUp. That was it. Too much of his story wasn't online.

She could walk right up Main to Treanor's right now and ask him what his story was herself. But no— that was a terrible idea. Back when she was in high school, she'd been so strongly attracted to him. They had been best friends only for that first year and a half, and she'd had to work pretty hard to keep herself from pushing for more. It was probably a good thing he'd left, because she'd never have been able to get over him and move on if he'd stuck around.

It was a little alarming that, after all these years, the attraction was just as strong. But this time it was going to be a piece of cake to keep herself from pushing for more. In high school, she held back because she hadn't wanted to ruin the beautiful friendship they'd had. Now, she held back for reasons that were so much stronger. Now she had experience on her side. That experience told her exactly what that man could do to her heart, so she knew to keep it well protected. She was going to have to get through this decorating quickly, so she could put some distance between her and him.

Chapter Four

At the end of the Main Street Business Alliance meeting, the only thing Eli's mom's text had said was *Your dad needs you here. How quickly can you get to the hospital?* Nothing about how he was doing. So of course Eli's mind went to every worst case scenario as he drove the thirty minutes to St. Anthony's.

After making his way to the information desk then through the hospital to where his dad was recovering, he finally took in a deep breath when he heard his dad's voice coming from his room. It was a croaky voice, but not as strained as he had feared. He stopped outside the room for a moment to calm his heart and his breathing before stepping into the doorway where he could be seen.

His dad lay on the bed in his hospital gown, an IV still in his arm, a blood pressure cuff around his arm, and an oxygen sensor on his finger. His mom sat on the opposite side of the bed from the equipment, holding his hand. They stopped talking when they saw him, and his mom stood up and hurried to him. She wrapped her arms around him, pinning his arms to his side. He managed to awkwardly pat her back with his fingertips.

"Hi, Mom."

She put her hands on his cheeks. "You're looking so grown up and handsome, son. We're so glad you are here, aren't we, Robert?"

Eli's dad grunted and pushed with his elbow, adjusting his shoulders on the bed. "I was wondering when you were going to get here."

"Hey, Dad," Eli said. "Other than being a bit pale, you're looking good. Surgery went well?" It had been a full four years since they'd last come to visit him in Sacramento, and the truth was, the extra wrinkles they both sported had caught him off guard just a bit, but they both looked good.

"As good as it can when a doctor cuts open your ankle, files off the ends of your broken bones, makes your own blood into a glue to stick it back together and puts in a couple of rods for good measure, and then makes you stay in this blasted bed with all these blasted cords attached everywhere."

"I see the surgery hasn't dampened your spirits at all." His mom playfully punched him in the arm, to show that she understood that he was joking. He wasn't. His dad still had his trademark "Treanor fire." Eli turned to his mom. "You didn't say what the problem was in your text. Is everything okay?"

She sat down on the bed and wrapped her hand in his dad's. His dad smiled and squeezed her hand back. Why couldn't they have been like this when he was in high school? Back then they didn't hold hands— they fought nightly until they finally decided to be separated for his junior and senior year, and neither of them was better for it. Now if he hadn't known better, he'd have guessed they had a textbook blissful marriage.

"Everything's fine. They said that the surgery went well. They were able to fully repair the damage. They expect recovery to be slow, but that's normal for this kind of surgery. I texted because once your father was awake from the anesthesia, he was anxious to talk with you about the business."

He should've guessed that's why his mom asked for him to come. Of course. Now that she'd said it, he wondered how he ever thought it could've been something different.

"Now I don't need to remind you that I built this business from the ground up," his dad said. "It's been my life for the past thirty-two years."

"Don't worry, Dad," Eli said in what he hoped was a reassuring voice. "I was only in town for a few minutes, but I had a good long phone call with the shift supervisor—"

"Grace," his mom supplied.

"Yes, and things have been going great today. You've trained her well, and I'll—"

"There's more to running a business than checking in with the shift supervisor," his dad said. "There's all the building maintenance and managing the employees and the accounting software and equipment upkeep and purchasing and advertising and customer relations."

Eli worked to keep his breathing even. A few months after he had escaped to California with nothing more than his car and the things he'd packed in his trunk, he'd called his mom from a payphone to say that he was okay. Eli hadn't been remotely prepared to be on his own, in a state where he knew no one. Both his parents had flown to the general area they'd figured out from the number on their caller ID, and found him at his lowest—sleeping in his car, showering at the local gym, flipping burgers for minimum wage, and about as far as possible from being the upstanding college student they'd wanted. In a heated argument over what he should've been doing with his life, his dad had said, "I didn't raise a low-life worthless bum. I no longer consider you my son," before flying back home.

Eli had come a long way since those first couple of years on his own. He was proud of what he'd made of his life. But whenever he was around his dad, it felt as if he still saw him as that same stupid, stubborn kid who made every bad choice possible. "I've got this, Dad. You don't have anything to worry about. I've run my own successful business for years now, you know."

"This isn't a business where you just get everyone to hold hands and sing Kumbaya! This is a *real* business, and it takes a *real* businessman to run it."

Heat rushed through Eli, making his breathing quicken and his hands sweat. "Why did you ask me to come here, Dad?"

"Because I... I don't know. I shouldn't have had this stupid operation. My ankle was fine enough before. I just need to get out of here so I can go take care of things at the shop like I always have."

The machine next to his dad started beeping, and his mom put a hand on his dad's arm. "Now calm down, Robert. Remember? The doc said to not do anything that will get your blood pressure up."

A nurse rushed in just then, hurrying to check the numbers on the machine. She pressed the button for the blood pressure cuff to start, and turned to them. "I'm going to have to ask you to leave for a minute while I take care of Mr. Treanor here."

"No problem at all," Eli said as he turned and left the room.

"Eli," his mom called out, stopping him in his tracks a few feet down the hall. He turned slowly to face her. "Now you know your dad didn't mean all that."

"I'm pretty sure he did."

"He's just frustrated that his body is getting older and forcing him to slow down. He loves that business, and just wishes he could be there, taking care of it."

"I get it. The man only has so much love to give."

"He loves you. He does. He just struggles to show it."

Eli knew it was pointless to argue otherwise with his mom. He also knew it was pointless to believe her. It had been a very long time since Eli was the kind of son that deserved his dad's love. "When you go back in, you can tell him that he doesn't need to worry. I'm going to take good care of Treanor's."

His mom smiled and wrapped an arm around him, giving him a side hug. "You're a good son."

"Oh, and tell him that I wish him a speedy recovery. Like inhumanly speedy. The kind that will make them write an article for the medical journals."

She let out a chuckle that broke the tension, and made Eli give a quick chuckle, too.

"It's good to have you back. I hope we get you for longer than you're hoping to be here."

Eli returned his mom's hug and then left. He hoped his mom didn't get her wish. Because too many things seemed too much like they were before he left so long ago.

He took a deep breath as he got in his car and headed back onto the freeway. He was a different person now, and things were going to turn out differently this time. It was going to start with his dad's business.

After parking in the lot behind Treanor's, Eli walked around to the front of the shop, then decided he was too close and walked to the middle of the pedestrian bridge that went over Snowdrift Springs. He stared at the building, imagining it through the eyes of a customer, looking for anything that might turn them away.

Sounds of group laughter took his gaze to the outdoor tables at the restaurant two buildings down. There were normally tables for five separate groups, but they were all pushed together into one large group. It looked like a mix of couples, families, high school friends and— he squinted— right in the middle of all of them was a very animated Whitney, telling some story that had them all enthralled.

Back in high school, it felt like this entire town didn't like the two of them. He had never been able to understand how anyone could've not liked Whitney. But now it appeared that the town had finally figured it out. The thought brought a smile to his face. And for some reason, it brought to mind Ben's conversation about Eli finding someone to date for longer than his self-imposed two week limit.

He let the smile fall from his face. Ben was wrong. He wasn't going to date anyone, and he definitely wasn't going to date Whitney. He hadn't stepped foot in this town for twelve years, so he hadn't done anything that would make them change their opinion about him, and he didn't want to drag any of that Whitney's direction. Besides, after the way he handled things when he left all those years ago, there was no way she would ever date him again anyway.

He was here to do exactly one thing. Make his dad proud by running his business well.

Oh, yeah. And plan the decorations for Fall Market.

Chapter Five

Whitney checked her appearance in the mirror of the bathroom at the Gazette. She twisted a curl that looked out of place, tucked one side of her hair behind her ear, applied new lipstick, smoothed down her shirt that read *More Style than the AP*, and straightened the front of her blazer. Then she dropped her hands to her sides and rolled her eyes at herself. Why was she checking to make sure everything was perfect just because Eli had texted, just like he'd promised, and she'd told him to meet her at the storage unit? She wasn't the type of girl to primp. She got ready in the morning, and didn't even glance in the mirror again all day. She did *not* care how she looked when she saw Eli again. Not at all. He was just someone she used to know who she still happened to be mad at.

She walked the block and a half down Main Street to City Hall, got the key to the storage unit from Gloria, the woman at the front desk, where Mayor Stone, one of the council members, and a police officer all stood chatting. She asked Officer Banks how his daughter was— "giving them a run for their money," apparently, and they all joked about how they did the same with their parents. After saying goodbye, she headed around the corner to Pack It In storage. Eli was already there, leaning against the door to the unit, reading something on his phone, looking like a page out of a magazine.

She glanced down at her watch. She was never late! She glanced back up right as he did, and she called out, "I'm so sorry— I guess I socialized at City Hall longer than I realized."

Apparently that was amusing to him, based on the crooked smile that took her right back to high school.

After unlocking the door, she pushed the key into her pocket and hefted the door open. Eli flipped the light switch, and they both stood there for a moment, staring at the stacks and stacks of cardboard boxes, plastic totes, large plastic-covered items— some that towered up to the ceiling— and wobbly stacks of things in plastic bags.

"Whoa," Eli breathed. "Is this the burial ground of festivals past? Are we standing on hallowed ground?"

Whitney smiled. "Nope— it's the birthplace of festivals future."

"Oh, so that's what the smell is," Eli said, coughing at the dust. "Hope, possibilities, and," he turned his head to the side as he looked up at a 15 foot replica of the Statue of Liberty, "moderation."

"And three month old fries," Whitney said as she picked up a bag with the Keetch's Burgers and Shakes logo, containing the remains of someone's lunch— probably Donald's from the Fourth of July celebration— and made a bee-line for the garbage can just outside the door. When she came back in, she took off her blazer and slung it over one of the boxes. She noticed his smile when he read her shirt. It shouldn't have made her heart tingle, but it did. She brushed away the feeling, pulled the clipboard out of her bag and said, "Okay, our first step is to go through all this stuff and make a list of the things we might be able to use. Then we'll meet again and make a plan of how to do the decorations. Sound good?"

Eli nodded. "Start at the back corner, and move our way to the front?" He led the way through the maze of objects, stopping to hold up some long floral stems that had fallen across the makeshift aisle, like they were following an animal trail through undergrowth in the mountains.

When they reached the back corner, Whitney looked down at her clipboard, then set it on a stack of boxes and turned around, leaning against the boxes. "I'm pretty sure we can be cordial to each other with the best of them. But maybe we should think about addressing the elephant in the room."

Eli reached up, petting the air, and said, "Hello, Elephant." Then he took a deep breath, like he was bracing himself.

No, not bracing himself. Closing himself off. Whitney pushed forward anyway. "Graduation night, twelve years ago. What happened?"

Shrugging, Eli said, "What can I say? I was a stupid kid."

Whitney took a deep, steadying breath. "Agreed. But what about the months after? The years after?"

"Stupid kid, stupid adult," Eli said, writing invisible checkmarks in the air.

Whitney studied him. There was a definite storm brewing beneath the surface— she should've known better than to hit it head on and expect an answer right off the bat after all this time, when an answer hadn't come at all in the past twelve years. Fine. He was going to be here a while; she'd just have to keep trying. She picked up the clipboard, and, still looking at it, said, "How's your dad?"

"Recovering. Fighting. Still just as ornery. His doctor told him he won't sign off on him going back to run the business for at least four to six weeks. Six is most likely for a surgery like his, but there's no way my dad will let the doc keep him a day past the minimum."

"He's a good guy, your dad. I know he has impossible expectations for you, but he's a good guy, deep down. He treats his customers well and does a lot for the community. He's more social than he used to be, too."

Eli gave her a look that she couldn't quite understand, so she said, "What?"

"I just hadn't ever thought about the fact that you would know my dad better than I do."

"Have you seen them at all in the past twelve years?" She suddenly realized that she wasn't sure how she would feel knowing that answer— would it make her more sad to know he had no contact with his parents either, or if he did, but still never made contact with her? She turned her back on him and opened the first box she saw.

"They come for a short visit every four years or so. My mom calls about once a month."

"It looks like all these boxes are for Easter." She turned to the next stack without making eye contact with Eli. She didn't know what expression was on her face, and didn't want to know what was on Eli's.

"Easter here, too."

"Of course some things from other holidays might work for us. Let's not rule anything out."

"Oh good," Eli said, pulling something yellow and fluffy out of a tote. "Because I would really like to see you in this 'fall' bunny costume." He reached over and placed the bunny ears on her head.

She twitched her nose like a bunny. "Deal. But only if you dress up as a 'fall' elf."

He laughed and took the bunny ears back off her head. "Maybe we better keep Easter right here where it belongs."

"Oh! The archways!" Whitney made her way around a couple tall piles of boxes to where six metal arches stood that were each nearly ten feet tall and six feet wide. "I don't think those have been used since... Founder's Day maybe five years ago. And that was in the park. I'm not sure they've ever been used for Fall Market. She whipped around to face Eli. "We have to find a way to use these."

He smiled at her enthusiasm. And even though she was still mad at him, things automatically slipped into a comfort level like back when they were in high school— for the first year and a half, when they were best friends, before they started dating—like they didn't know how to act otherwise.

They went through all the boxes and totes, unwrapping big objects just enough to see what they were, and opening bags of supplies, writing down everything that could possibly be used for a fall celebration.

"We haven't checked the boxes in that corner," Whitney said. "Those are part of the banners for the Fourth, but those two boxes over there are promising. I can feel it in my bones." Whitney scooted as close as she could to the stacked boxes that were blocking her path, but she couldn't reach far enough to get them without falling face down on the boxes.

Eli picked up a box from the stack. "I can move these out of the way."

"Nah," Whitney said. "There's no good place to move them. Grab hold of my ankle." She planted her right leg right against a box and lifted her left leg out behind her, balancing on her right. Eli gave her a questioning look, but she just shook her leg and said, "Ankle."

He grabbed her ankle with both hands and she leaned forward, no longer worried about her center of gravity making her fall if she reached too far. "Lower me in further," she said, her breath coming out in a whoosh as she leaned over boxes. Eli moved forward with her ankle, allowing her to reach far enough to grab the box. "Got it! Reel me in!"

Eli slowly pulled her leg backward, and she set the box down on the stack in front of her. When she was mostly upright, he released her ankle, but she stepped down on a wayward carnival rubber ducky and lost her balance, falling right into Eli.

"Don't worry, I've got you," he said, wrapping his hands around her waist to steady her.

Her hands had landed on his strong chest, and his familiar scents of fabric softener and deodorant hit her. But now there was another scent, too— something musky and amazing that zinged through her, making her heart race while feeling light-headed. Without thinking first, she said as her hands rested on his chest, "Yep. Definitely not still eighteen."

As soon as the words came out of her mouth, heat rushed up her body and she was sure that her face and neck were even redder than her hair. His crooked smile turned into a full ear to ear one, which made her more embarrassed.

She picked up her clipboard and fanned herself, trying to cool the blush. "When did it get so hot in here? Is it hot in here? I think it's hot."

"No, that's just you."

Whitney laughed, the sound bouncing off the walls and totes in the room. In her best announcer voice, she said, "And the cheesiest line of the day goes to... Eli Treanor!"

Eli joined her laughing. "Blast from the past right there. I had forgotten we used to say that."

Whitney had forgotten how much she had missed just hanging out with Eli. She cleared her throat. "So, did you volunteer to help with the business while your dad recovered?"

"Ha. No. Volunteer to come remind my dad daily how disappointed in me he is? No."

Right. He was only here to put in his time until he could race away, like when he was in high school. Just like before, the attraction was there any moment she spent with him. But she wasn't going to let a little thing like attraction punch holes in her carefully crafted walls. If there was anyone in the world who was a pro at keeping things at a friend level when his magnetism was pulling her in more, it was Whitney Brennan. She didn't let emotions or a certain person's attractiveness sway her. Logic was her best friend. It saved her every time.

She looked down at her watch and gasped. "I had no idea we'd been here so long," she said as she rushed back to the front and grabbed her blazer. "I've got to get back to the paper to finish my articles and get started on layouts. My employees are going to be there any second now, and I haven't even gotten my parts started."

"And my shift manager is leaving in twenty. I've got to go take her place."

"We'll get together soon to plan," she said as she locked the door and waved a goodbye to a man who was much too attractive for her own good. She was grateful for the cooler temperatures as she rushed the direction of City Hall to return the key.

Chapter Six

When Eli got back to Treanor's Outdoor Rentals, the place was crowded with several families who had come at the same time. He apologized to Grace for not getting back to help out sooner, and the two of them worked together to get most of them helped before Grace had to skip out. It took a good thirty minutes after she left to get the last customer out the door with their paddle boards and oars.

It had been exhilarating having so many customers in at the same time, and he wished it was like that all the time. He grabbed a notepad and pen from the office, and started brainstorming ideas to get more customers while he was wandering around the store, straightening the *For Sale* racks of swim suits, jackets, hats, sunglasses, and inflatable water toys.

Most tourists stayed in either the same hotel he was staying in, Home Suite Home, or at All Nestled Inn, the other hotel in town. Maybe he could get both of them to let him put up a display that would get visitors dying to try out the local outdoor activities to head to Treanor's. He should advertise the discount they had for locals more, too. The locals lived right in the middle of this beautiful outdoors that surrounded them. It shouldn't be something that only the tourists enjoyed. That's where he would be right now if he weren't working— outside using some of this equipment. Playing on the lake or in the mountains or biking on the trails.

Maybe he could put an ad in the Nestled Hollow Gazette. If things were like they used to be— and he was sure they were — then practically every home in Nestled Hollow had a subscription to the paper. A lot of people would often buy a second copy just so they could save an article that had theirs or a loved one's name and picture in it. It would be the perfect place to advertise to the locals.

The excitement of moving a business forward had apparently made him think of TeamUp, because before he even realized he'd thought of it, his phone was in his hand, calling Ben. He answered on the second ring.

"Hey," Eli said. "I didn't actually think you'd be able to answer. Don't you have a group today?" He steered one of the tandem bikes from the showroom floor and drove it out front so people could see it when they drove by.

"They're getting snacks and glaring at each other right now."

"That group of managers from Mauldin Metrics?"

"Yep. Never seen a group of people more competitive with each other. No, wait. Remember the human resource department from Cropton Property Management? So we've had it this bad before."

Eli laughed and headed back into the store to grab a paddle board. Some groups came to them in pretty dysfunctional shape. It was one of the main reasons why companies would pay to have them spend a day or two or five at TeamUp.

"Don't worry. By time you're done with them, they'll be doing as great as Cropton was at the end, too."

"Travis is a good kid, but he's much more suited to being our runner. He doesn't have your gift for pulling people together. This is going to be a tough one. Oh, by the way, StylesTech couldn't say enough good about you."

"Stop. You're making me homesick." He leaned the paddle board against the building, just behind the bike.

"You're home. You can't be homesick."

"You know Sacramento is home much more than this place ever was."

"So what I'm hearing is that you're having a grand time."

"The best." Eli didn't even need to use a sarcastic tone. Ben would understand even without it. He grabbed the smaller rolling rack of life jackets and put them out front, too.

"I meant what I said about dating—I want you coming back heartbroken. When was the last time you were? Not since I've known you. It's good for the soul, I hear."

Like he was going to let himself go home broken-hearted. He didn't think he could take getting his heart broken by the same girl twice. "What I'm hearing is that the California sun is doing some damage to your senses."

Ben laughed a booming laugh. "I'm just saying. Oh! Gotta go. Looks like someone might start throwing individually wrapped packages of Cheeze-Its and Rice Krispy Treats if I don't get these guys separated and doing something constructive."

"Good luck," Eli said, then hung up and put his phone in his pocket.

He spent the next hour crafting a sandwich board that read "Rent Me" to put outside by the equipment, and looking up every time a customer walked through the door, hoping it was

Whitney. Which was stupid, because he didn't want to see her. He'd been in love with her for so long, getting over her had hurt. Okay, if he was being honest, he hadn't ever gotten over her, so it all still hurt. He had enough flaws to know that he wasn't the right person for her, but that wasn't enough to stop his heart, apparently.

He pulled out his phone and started a text to her. Then, without sending it, he put his phone back in his pocket. She deserved better than him.

Whenever no customers were in the shop, he went back to the bikes, checking the tire pressure, pumping them up when needed, and greasing the chains. It was something he'd done so often, though, it didn't take much brainpower, leaving his mind free to think about Whitney. About her infectious smile. The way she made him laugh. Holding onto her ankle and working as a team to get that unreachable box. He laughed out loud, all alone in the store, when he realized they'd never actually opened that box. Then he thought about how it had felt to have her hands on his chest and his hands on her waist when she fell into him. About the look on her face. She'd felt something too, he was certain.

The phone was back in his hand. They had a responsibility to meet to discuss the decorations. They had a job to do. He wasn't texting her because he wanted to date her. This was strictly business.

PLANNING, PHASE II. TOMORROW?

He backspaced over the text and tried again.

WE'VE GOT TWO WEEKS UNTIL FALL MARKET, RIGHT? WE BETTER GET CRACKIN'.

Awful. He deleted again.

Nothing spells "Success in Fall Market decoration planning" quite like Keetch's. (And the cheesiest line of the day goes to...) Lunch tomorrow?

Still not perfect. He made himself punch the send button with his pointer finger before he could delete and try again though.

There. He was doing the same thing he did in high school — taking her places filled with people and noise and chaos, so she wouldn't have a clue he was interested in anything more than living in the friend zone.

Chapter Seven

*W*hitney stood at one end of the printing press in the room connected to the office. In a pinch, she could probably run the presses herself, but Tony had been doing it since the dawn of time, and knew everything about running and maintaining the machines. And he never missed a day. He had even been around when the very first edition of the paper had been printed, back when Mr. Annesley had started the Nestled Hollow Gazette.

As she waited for the machines to spin to life, she pulled out her phone to tell Brooke about the storage shed today, and then remembered that she was on a plane. Brooke being gone was just a little thing— she'd be back eventually. But it scared her that she had gotten to the point with Brooke where she wanted to call her to tell her about something going on in her life. Everyone always left. It wasn't worth getting close to anyone— that only came with hurt. And Brooke always left as often as most people did their laundry, so she shouldn't want to be sharing anything with her. It was all because Eli had gotten her to let her guard down. At least she caught herself quickly enough.

She didn't need to be here for this part of the newspaper creation process— Tony was good about getting the papers to the cadre of twelve to fifteen-year-olds who showed up on bikes and delivered the papers everywhere in town. But she came in here for the printing every single time because it spoke to her soul. There was something about the whirring of the roll of paper being sent through the printers, the rhythmic click of the papers being cut, and the *chonk chonk thrip* of the papers being folded that made everything they'd written real. Concrete.

A beep sounded that wasn't from the machines. She pulled her cell phone out and saw a text from Eli, asking to meet her at Keetch's for lunch tomorrow.

Part of her wanted to reply with something joking, like *As long as their A/C is working. ;)*

But no. She wasn't going to willingly walk into danger. She typed in *Sure. 1:00?* and touched send.

Guard: fully raised.

Whitney hated cooking at her apartment unless she had people over. The way she saw it, her apartment served three purposes: sleeping, getting ready for the day, and having people over. If it didn't fit into one of those three, she wasn't interested in being there. Which meant she ate at places in town a lot. She ate at Keetch's a lot, in fact. She'd made plenty of memories in this place over the past twelve years. Yet the moment she walked in and saw Eli at their normal table right by the front windows, all the memories of this place that she could think of involved him.

She straightened her blazer to give herself a chance to peek down at her shirt which read *Be BOLD and give 'em Helvetica*, like seeing it would make her feel it more. *Guard. Fully. Raised*, she reminded herself in her fiercest voice. She took a deep breath, until she could feel in her bones that this was a business lunch only, and then went to the table.

"Hello, Eli." She even gave him a warm, professional smile as she slid into the other seat at the table.

"Hi, Whitney." He gave her his crooked, mischievous smile.

One of the teenaged waitresses came over just then, Christy, and said "What can I get for you?"

Whitney thought for a moment, and said, "Let's do the bacon burger and fries today."

As Christy was writing, she said out lout, "Bacon cheeseburger, no onion or pickle, fries, and a water. And for you, sir?"

The faintest amused smile quirked the side of Eli's mouth, and he said, "The same for me, except with extra pickles." He handed Christy the two menus that neither of them had touched.

Whitney pulled a manila folder out of her bag and opened it on the table. "Here's the list of items we found in the storage shed. And oh— I went back to the storage shed and looked in those last few boxes that we didn't check before we left. They were filled with garlands of fall leaves, so that could be helpful. I've added them to the list. And I printed out several black and white copies of a picture I took of Main Street a while ago and brought sharpies, so we can draw right on them to get a better idea of how it will look."

"So we're going straight into the planning, then," Eli said.

Whitney didn't let herself take the slightest moment to try

to interpret the look on his face. "That's what we're here for, right? We both have businesses to run and the Fall Market is in two short weeks. Saturdays are generally busy days, and I figure neither of us have time to waste."

"Okay, then. Let's get to it."

By the time their food arrived, they had already drawn on three of the copies of Main Street. One had fall-colored buntings hung beneath the windows on each of the buildings, with fall garlands wrapped around the guard rails of the pedestrian bridges. One had the six archways they'd found placed right at both openings of each of the pedestrian bridges, with the fall garlands draped over them, with pumpkins and bundles of dried cornstalks placed in groups at several locations. And one had bales of hay placed in groups, with fall fabric on top so people could sit and socialize.

They both picked up their burgers and took a bite, staring at the drawings, thinking in silence. Whitney picked up the list of items that were in the storage unit, and read through it again as she munched on fries. Eventually, she said, "The problem is, there aren't many decorations for the Fall Market. It's never been done well. There's some money in the budget to buy new things, but not much."

"Do you already have something in mind to buy?" Eli said as he folded his paper napkin, then turned it over and made more folds.

Whitney shrugged. "A giant wreath for the bell tower? I don't know."

"The problem is," Eli said, still messing with his napkin while Whitney looked at the list, hoping something would eventually pop out at her, "everything we've come up with is generic. These decorations could go in any town across America. They aren't specific to Nestled Hollow."

Then he held the paper napkin out to Whitney— folded into the shape of a swan, with the Keetch's Burgers and Shakes logo perfectly centered on the side— and her breath caught in her throat. She cupped her palms, and he placed it right in the middle of them, her heart racing. Then she carefully set it on the table and ran a finger down the neck of the swan, making sure not to bend the napkin. "I kept the first one of these you ever gave me." Eli's gaze whipped from the swan to her face, but Whitney just kept staring at the swan. "I put it on my dresser, front and center, and it stayed there for a good year and a half. It didn't survive the move into my college dorm, but I still couldn't bring myself to throw it out until I moved back here."

She looked up at him, but couldn't read the expression on his face before he cleared his throat and turned to look out the front window. She looked out the window, too, and tried to get her attention back on the project.

"We aren't going to figure this out in here. We need to go up there." Eli held his arm out, palm up, toward the ski lift that went from the edge of town, just a few blocks away, and rose up the mountain. The entire mountainside had been turning brilliant shades of yellows, oranges, and reds over the past week. "We can ride the ski lift to the top, and be right in the middle of fall while overlooking the entire town, and I bet we'd get some inspiration that would be more unique to Nestled Hollow. You can bring your camera— you'd get some great shots of the town you could probably use for a story."

Whitney glanced down at the swan, then back at the striking mountain that was practically kissing the town's back door, then down at the pictures of Main Street that they'd drawn on. She wasn't happy with anything they'd come up with so far, and it suddenly felt like all the answers were up there. She looked over at Eli and grinned. "Let's do it."

"After church tomorrow? I'll pack a picnic dinner, if you'll bring a blanket. I doubt the Home Suite Home would appreciate me bringing the one off the bed there."

Whitney laughed. "Probably not. Tomorrow it is."

Eli pulled his phone out of his pocket, looked at the screen for a moment, and then said, "The store's too busy for Grace and Max to handle on their own. I've got to go." He got out his wallet and left money for lunch on the table. He took a breath, like he was about to say something, and then hesitated. After a moment, he just said, "See you tomorrow," then hurried out the door.

Whitney could still hear the voice in her head telling her to raise her guard because it had slipped a bit, but she just kept running her finger down the neck of the swan, her mind going back to every Friday night as teenagers when they'd come here, and he'd fold her a swan. Eventually, she put all the papers back into the folder and slid them into her bag, then carefully scooped up the swan to take back to her office. For old time's sake.

Chapter Eight

*E*li showed up at the church five minutes late and slid into a seat at the back of the congregation. The truth was, he'd only been inside a church a handful of times since leaving Nestled Hollow. But going to church on Sundays was what he did back when he lived here, so it just felt natural to go. And if he was being even more honest, he'd admit that Whitney was a much bigger reason why he went. Most of the time he'd been around her, she'd been distant. Cautious. But there were a couple of times when things felt more natural between them, and it made him want to be around her even more.

He scanned the congregation, and found her four rows from the front, in the middle of the bench, surrounded by people, making faces at a toddler who bounced on her lap. Of course that's where he'd find her— right in the middle of the people. Maybe he was making a mistake wanting to see her more. The town loved her. Him, not so much. He didn't want to bring her down.

When the meeting closed, he realized he hadn't paid attention to anything the pastor had said. He'd heard of people having amazing experiences when going back to church for the first time after a long absence, but apparently he was a little too rusty. He'd have to come ready to focus next time, if that was even possible. Maybe he'd have to sit behind someone super tall so he couldn't see Whitney if he wanted to.

While everyone headed out onto the lawn for a potluck and socializing, Eli slipped away. He'd have leaped at a gathering like that back in Sacramento, but there were too many old-timers here who would probably appreciate it if he didn't stay.

Besides, he had a picnic dinner to prepare.

He was a passable cook, but he couldn't make something that would need to stay warm for their trip up into the mountains. Plus, there was the added complication that the only kitchen appliances his hotel room had were a mini fridge, a microwave, and a coffee maker. But using mostly pre-cooked ingredients from Elsmore Market, he made a mean turkey bacon avocado sandwich on focaccia bread, if he did say so himself. He'd also bought a veggie tray and dip, a few different types of chips, and, right at the end, he threw in a couple of mint brownies, because if he remembered correctly, Whitney was a fan. He bought ice packs and an overpriced fabric cooler from his parents' store, and stuffed the ice packs in the three inch high section of his mini fridge dedicated to freezer space.

At 4:00, Eli arrived at the ski lift and Whitney was already there, chatting with the man at the base of the lift. She was wearing the same outfit she'd been wearing at church— a mid-length denim skirt, dark brown boots that went up to her knees, a dark brown vest, and a deep orangish brown shirt that brought out the auburn in her hair and made her face radiant. A quilt was folded over one arm and a bag slung over one shoulder, and when she saw him coming, he could swear he saw her face brighten. He had all the fall inspiration he needed right there.

"Hi, Eli," she said as he neared. "You remember Don Anderson, right?"

Eli nodded—Don was the father of a guy he'd been friends with since the fifth grade— and shook Don's hand. "Good to see you again."

"You too," Don said. "Been staying out of trouble?"

Eli bristled. Everyone always assumed he was being a troublemaker. It had been a long time since high school. He tried not to let it show and just said, "Yes, sir."

"Tell your dad hello from me. He's a good guy—he's helped me out of a pinch more than once. I hope his recovery goes well."

"Will do."

Don looked up the mountainside. "This is a slow time of year, and there's not a lot of people I'd make a special trip out here on a Sunday to start the lift for, but by golly, Whitney's one of them. I'll make sure you get to the top. There's a cell tower on that ridge right there, so you should have reception. Just give me a call when you're ready to come back down."

"You're one of the best there is, Don," Whitney said.

"That's what I want my headline to say," Don said, winking, and then letting out a rumbling laugh. "Now you two kids go have fun and get lots of ideas."

Don started the ski lift, and Whitney and Eli stood on the spot marked on the ground, and hopped onto a seat as it came around to them.

"It didn't even occur to me that the ski lift wouldn't be running right now," Eli said. "Thanks for working your magic with Don."

"It's the least I could do after you volunteered to bring dinner." She flashed him a smile that made his heart jump.

Eli loved Sacramento for so many reasons. But as the lift rose up the mountain and the fall leaves exploded with color all around him, he couldn't remember why he'd ever been in such a hurry to leave a place like this.

Whitney shuffled the blanket to the side, and then pulled her camera out of her bag and took off the lens cap, pushing it into her vest pocket. She started taking pictures of the fall leaves on her side of the lift, then a group of trees off Eli's side caught her attention, and she leaned that way to get the picture. She kept taking more, adjusting slightly, until she was leaning with her arm brushing against Eli's. She smelled amazing— like cherry blossoms. He didn't know how long it had been since he'd last smelled cherry blossoms, and before that moment, he wouldn't have thought that he even know what they smelled like, but he was convinced that was what the smell was.

She finished taking shots and straightened back up. "How did you like the sermon today?"

"You saw me?"

She pulled the lens cover out of her pocket and put it on the camera, then slid the camera into her bag. "I saw you sneaking out the back before the luncheon."

"It's not really my scene."

"Unless I'm thinking of some other Eli Treanor, it's totally your scene."

Eli looked out across the sea of trees.

Whitney sucked in a quick breath of air then nodded slowly. "You flinched."

"I what?"

"When Don asked if you were staying out of trouble, you flinched."

He'd hoped it hadn't been obvious. "You do remember one of the reasons why I wanted to get out of here right after high school, right? The people in this town don't like me a whole lot." He had been going for a light, joking voice, but he could hear the bit of bitterness that crept in. He hoped Whitney hadn't noticed. But Whitney always noticed.

"That was twelve years ago."

"And you heard Don— they still think I'm a troublemaker."

Whitney laughed. He hadn't remembered her laugh being so musical. Then she turned in her seat, one leg bent, took his hand in hers, and looked him in the eyes. Just like she used to do when she really wanted him to pay attention to what she was about to say. Eli wasn't sure he could pay attention because all he could think about was how Whitney was holding his hand and her leg was touching his, and it felt like electricity was zinging up his arm.

"Remember back when we thought everyone in town hated us?"

Eli nodded. Like it was yesterday.

"They didn't. It took me a while to realize it, too, but they weren't mad— they saw two teenagers who had lost their fathers— mine permanently to cancer and yours temporarily to failing marriage-induced drinking and separation from your mom. They were worried about us. Concerned that the stupid ways we were coping were going to ruin our futures. It wasn't the last hardship this town has seen me through. It was during the next one that I really understood that they were trying to help. I know this town well. Trust me: they don't hate you."

Eli shrugged and looked back out at the trees. He absolutely believed that. For her. For himself— well, he'd believe it when he saw it. She turned back to the front, and he glanced back over at her. He wondered what the next hardship she faced was. It sounded like there was even more than that. But by the look on her face, she wasn't ready for him to ask. And besides, if he did, she'd probably want more answers from him, and he wasn't ready, either.

Whitney picked up the blanket as they neared the end of the lift. Then the lift jerked to a stop, making their car rock back and forth. They both turned to look behind them, as if they'd be able to see what was wrong.

"Did he think we already made it to the top?" Eli asked.

Whitney shook her head. "He has binoculars."

Her phone rang just then, and she answered it. After a moment of one word responses, she said, "Okay, thanks, Don." Then she ended the call and turned to him. "Mechanical problem. He's going to try to fix it, but he's guessing he might need to call someone to come in. He said it could be a couple of hours." Her brow furrowed. "And the end is right there," she said, motioning with both hands for emphasis.

Eli leaned forward, looking down at the ground, and then looked back at Whitney, grinning. "Wanna jump down? It's only like six feet."

"Are you serious? Jump?" She leaned forward, looking down at the ground, a nervous expression on her face.

"Well, not 'jump' so much as lower ourselves down and drop. It'll only be a couple of feet we'll have to fall. It'll just add to the adventure. Give us a story to tell."

Whitney bit her lip, the motion drawing Eli's eyes to them. "I'll catch you."

She hesitantly nodded. "Okay. If you're sure."

Eli smiled one of the most genuine smiles he'd had since arriving in Nestled Hollow. This was the kind of thing he did all the time with Ben at TeamUp. He'd felt off kilter and like he'd stepped back into high school for so much of the time he'd been here, but this made him feel like the real Eli just came back. He grabbed hold of the bars on the side of the car, swung his legs over the edge, dangled for just a moment, hanging from the cart, and then dropped to the ground. The angle of the mountain caused him to stumble a couple of steps, but he'd been close enough that he didn't fall.

"Now drop the stuff down to me."

Whitney grabbed the cooler by its strap, lowered it as far as she could reach, and then dropped it to him. He caught it easily, set it on the ground, and then raised his arms again. This time, he caught the blanket as she dropped it.

"I'm going to drop my bag with my camera down to you, but you've got to hold that blanket out like it's a trampoline and catch it in there, okay?"

Eli dutifully arranged the blanket for optimal bag catching. She held it out by its strap, and then pulled back a bit. "I'm serious; you have to catch this carefully, no matter what. Even at the cost of your own safety."

Eli chuckled.

"I'm serious, Eli. This is my camera, and it cost more than my car."

He adjusted the blanket enough to give her a Boy Scout salute, even though he'd dropped out before getting his Eagle. "On my honor, I swear I will not drop your camera."

She held the bag out again and dropped it this time, and it fell right into the cushion of the blanket. He made a show of setting it down as gently as humanly possible, away from where she was about to drop down herself. She did the same thing he'd done— held on to the bars at the side and swung her legs down. But then she screamed and kicked her legs wildly. "I changed my mind! I don't want to drop down!"

Eli grabbed at her legs at the knees, scooping them together. "I'm right here. I won't let you fall." She was up too high for him to grab around her waist, though, and knew she'd be off balance if he tried to just hold her with his arms wrapped around her knees. "I can keep holding on to your knees, and you can drop down to sitting on my shoulder, or I can let go of your knees and catch you in my arms. Which would you prefer?"

"Catch me in your arms," she said.

"One, two, three!"

Whitney let go, and Eli caught her, only taking a slight steadying step. Her arm immediately wrapped around his neck, and she breathed in fast, her face blushing with excitement.

"You good?" Eli asked.

Whitney let out an exhilarated laugh, her face inches away from his. "I clearly do not have enough excitement in my life when you're not around, Eli Treanor."

He set her down on the ground, handed the bag and then the blanket to her, and put the strap of the cooler over his shoulder. Then he wrapped his hand in hers and led her the twenty feet up the mountain, like it was no big deal that he was holding Whitney Brennan's hand once again.

Chapter Nine

*W*hitney regularly had dinner with a couple dozen families in town. She played after dinner games with them, each family having their own types of games, some indoor, some outdoor. She went out to eat and have fun with groups of singles in town. She hung out with the entire town at once with every celebration. She had meals with tourists and showed them around.

But she hadn't realized how much she missed this kind of fun. The Eli kind of fun. The kind where caution was thrown to the wind along with whatever plans they had, and spontaneity took over. At the landing area for the lift, she took in the fresh air and the view. If Eli had grabbed her hand again and said, "Let's climb over the crest of this mountain," she wouldn't have hesitated. She had that much energy.

"The view up here really is incredible, isn't it?" Eli stood at the edge of the flat area, looking out across the valley.

Whitney stepped up to him and looked out at how the mountain tops all around them looked like hills rising up, covered with greenish grays of evergreens and the deep, fall colors of the oaks, maples, and aspens. She took off her lens cap and brought her camera up, looking at the town through the lens, focusing in on Main Street, and snapping picture after picture. Something about seeing it from this height made it magical. Then she turned to the right a bit, and took pictures of the lake and the few people riding paddle boats on it. Sometimes, the worst thing about taking beautiful pictures of scenes with incredible color was knowing that when she put them in the paper, they'd all be printed in black and white.

She put the lens cap back on and turned around when Eli did.

"I guess we are now officially on the hunt for inspiration," he said, stepping away from the ski lift and onto the pathway skiers took to get to the top of the Silver Valley trail on the left. Then he turned up a pathway made by animals, Whitney following close behind. They had only been walking a few minutes when the thick underbrush opened up into a field of dry grasses surrounded by maple trees in the most vibrant oranges and yellows. A few of the leaves had fallen from the trees and onto the small field. Eli turned around to face her. "We need to close off Main Street."

"We... what?"

"Do you think we can get the Main Street Business Alliance to do it? There are other places to park, right?"

Whitney nodded slowly. "There's that big field just beyond Main. We could use that as a parking lot. Are you thinking we should make Main Street into a pedestrian mall for the day?" No one had ever done that before.

He spread his arms wide. "What about if we came up here right before the festival, when the leaves have finished changing color and are falling to the ground. We could gather them up, take them into town, and cover both sides of Main Street with them. You wouldn't even be able to tell that it was a normal street with parking spots and lines painted. It would look like up here."

"The Christmas lights," Whitney said, the excitement of all the possibilities practically exploding out of her. "We can ask Sam in facilities to hang them from the tops of the buildings on one side, spread all the way across Main Street to the buildings on the other side, just like at Christmastime. But before he does, we can hang fall leaves from them, dangling down at all different heights. Then it will look like the leaves are right in the middle of falling. Imagine how incredible that will look at night when they turn on the lights."

"It'd be amazing. And those arches you wanted to use," Eli said. "We've got six— we could place one at both openings of both the northbound and southbound sides, and use the other two where Center crosses through Main. Maybe weave through branches with fall leaves, and they could be the entrance into the Fall Market."

Whitney had a lightness in her chest making her feel like she was floating as she paced around the field, unable to stay still with so much energy coursing through her. "Campfires."

Eli stopped moving and looked at her.

"We need campfires. Fall Market always gets cold once the sun goes down, and so people aren't so willing to stay outdoors. If we got a bunch of campfires going, maybe get cut logs for people to sit on around the campfire and socialize, they'd stay longer. They'd get warm and shop for longer. There are enough people in town with those portable metal fire pits that I bet we could borrow."

Whitney spread the blanket on the ground, then sat down and pulled the folder out of her bag. She started drawing in all their ideas with the sharpie, and Eli scribbled all their ideas in a notebook as they came rapid fire. Before long, Eli had filled a page of notes, and Whitney had a drawing of Main Street that she knew would be a winner.

She held it up and they both grinned at it. "The credit for this goes to you. Coming up here to brainstorm was brilliant."

"The credit for dinner goes to me, too," he said as he pulled the cooler closer. "Are you hungry?"

"Starving." Whitney was surprised at how hungry she was — with all the brainstorming, she hadn't even noticed.

Eli pulled out all the food, and Whitney's mouth started watering. She bit into the turkey, bacon, and avocado sandwich seconds after Eli placed it in front of her, and before even swallowing, she moaned, "This is amazing."

He tossed her a bag of chips and winked. "Just give me a plastic knife, a microwave, and a mini fridge, and there's no telling what I can come up with."

Whitney swallowed her bite and said, "You didn't just go to your parents to make it?"

Eli gave an amused snort. "No." Then after a pause, he added, "But I guess I could have— they don't get home from the hospital until tomorrow. But breaking into their house would've been a little weird."

Whitney was trying to interpret his expressions, but not getting enough to really figure him out. She couldn't even guess which questions were okay to ask. So carefully, like she was approaching an injured animal, she asked with as much indifference as she could manage, "Have you been at the hospital much?"

He shook his head. "Just the day he had his surgery— the first day I was in town. But I've been getting text updates from my mom. Apparently he's driving the nursing staff crazy. They're just as ready for him to leave as he is."

"Your dad's a fighter. He'll be up and just as active before you know it."

"That's what *everyone's* hoping," Eli said, with two thumbs up and a grimace.

Whitney launched a carrot stick at him. He dodged, and launched a piece of broccoli in retaliation.

They both took a couple of bites in silence. Then Eli said, "I've got to go over and visit when they get settled back home tomorrow, though." After a beat, he said, "You should go with me."

Whitney held up one finger as she finished chewing a bite of her sandwich, unable to answer.

"My parents have always loved you. And if you go with me, my dad probably won't tell me I'm going to ruin his company. As much. Please. Say you'll come with me."

Whitney swallowed and laughed. "Okay, I'll go with you to visit your recovering father so that you won't get into trouble. As much."

They finished eating and cleaned up everything, but still the ski lift hadn't restarted. It was a beautiful day, though, so Whitney lay back on the blanket and stared up at the sky. A moment later, Eli lay down right beside her, and they both looked up at the big fluffy clouds.

"Right up there," Whitney said, pointing at a cloud. "That's an elephant, running on her hind legs. That jet stream is the ribbon at the finish line, and she's thrown her arms out because she's almost there and about to win."

Eli pointed up at a different cloud. "And that raccoon isn't too happy about it. That's the elephant's bag of peanuts right there, and he's pouring ants into it."

Staring up at the sky reminded Whitney of a time near the end of their senior year when they'd both been laying on a blanket, staring up at the stars. She'd felt just as peaceful and happy then.

She turned to her side, her head resting in her hand, propped up by her elbow. Eli turned her direction, mirroring her. For a moment, she allowed herself to just look at him and how he'd changed. The dark curls that used to fall free in a messy brilliance were now trimmed closer on the sides. It was still long enough on top to be fun, but the hair all fell into place as if this neater, more professional look was the way it meant to be all along. He had the full force of his icy blue eyes fixed on her, and she might as well have been in a trance for how hard it was to look away.

"Are you dating anyone?" Nice, Whitney. Nice and smooth. It came out sounding like she was about to ask him on a date or something, instead of out of pure curiosity like she'd meant it.

He raised an eyebrow, amused. "Nope. I'm not a fan. You?"

She should've seen that question coming. Maybe she should think before she asked questions all willy nilly. She decided to go for a simple, "No. I don't date." His brow crinkled, confused. He took a breath like he was about to ask why, but that answer was too complicated, and she wasn't about to get into it. So before he could ask, she threw her own question out there. "Why aren't you a fan of dating? Was there a serious relationship in your past that ended badly?" *Seriously, Whitney,* she scolded herself. *Way to ease in to the hard questions.*

He studied her, emotions crossing his face so quickly she

couldn't even name one before the next came. Still, he didn't take his eyes off hers. Eventually, he answered. "You can't get in a serious relationship if you limit yourself to dating each person for two weeks tops. Works out pretty well."

She had so many questions about that she wanted to ask. She wanted all the details. But instead of blurting out a question, she decided to learn from her last two mistakes and think first. Which gave him the opening he needed to ask her the next question first.

"What about you? Any serious relationships in your past that ended badly?"

She wasn't sure what expression, exactly, crossed her face, but his reaction told her it wasn't good. He looked like he might backtrack and tell her she didn't have to answer, but she plowed forward anyway. She'd rather answer this one than some others he could ask. "One. About a year out of college, I was engaged. We'd been together for nearly three years, but two months before we were supposed to be married, he decided that a job in New York was more important."

"Is that when you stopped dating?"

His expression was so full of concern, she wanted to reach out and put a hand on his cheek. Luckily, she stopped herself. "No. Not right then."

Instead of touching his cheek, she whacked him on the shoulder, knocking him over and causing him to yelp as he caught himself.

"Sorry! There was a huge bug on your shoulder!"

He righted himself and raised an eyebrow.

"I swear. Look— it's crawling off right over there. It's practically the size of a chipmunk!"

But he didn't turn to look. He just kept his eyes on hers, his eyebrow raised. His perfect eyebrow and those beautiful eyes.

His expression crinkled his forehead slightly and the corner of his mouth quirked up in the faintest smile. She could gaze at that face all day long and still not take it in enough.

The wind blew a lock of hair across her face, and he reached out and tucked it behind her ear, his hand lingering longer than needed, before grazing his fingertips down her neck, across her shoulder, and down her arm resting at her side. His touch sent electricity zinging a trail behind it and down her spine.

His eyes shifted from her eyes to her lips, which made her eyes fly to his lips. After being friends for so long in high school, they'd dated for four months before he left, and she never felt like she'd gotten enough time kissing those lips. Those lips that were just barely parted and looking so soft and inviting. She leaned in and he leaned in, her eyes back on his, taking in all the ice blue facets, their faces just inches away. She moved to close the last bit of distance when the ski lift whirred back to life.

They both turned their heads to the direction of the lift before turning back. It was enough, though, to break the spell, and Whitney leapt up.

What was she doing?

They needed to stop lying on blankets and staring up at the sky, because bad things happened when they did that. They had been going along just fine as friends for a year and five months, and it was a kiss on a blanket that changed everything, making his leaving so much more difficult. And here she was, almost allowing the same thing to happen. She paced a few steps, hands on her hips. "We've got to go."

She picked up her camera bag and ducked under the strap, not meeting his gaze, knowing he probably had a bewildered expression on his face. But with her brain all swirling and lightheaded and confused, she was unsure of what to do about that. Eli stood, his motions slow and careful as she gathered the blanket and slung it over an arm, not even bothering to fold it. He picked up the cooler, swung the strap over his shoulder, and they headed back down the trail to the tram.

Chapter Ten

*E*li tried to hide a yawn as he filled out a form for a couple of newlywed tourists who were renting a pair of mountain bikes and helmets. He shouldn't have lain awake in bed all night, thinking about his almost kiss with Whitney, about how it had felt to touch her skin or hold her hand. And he definitely shouldn't have replayed in his mind over and over that moment when she pulled away so quickly. Something had spooked her, but he couldn't guess what it might be. Maybe she'd just been caught up in the moment, and then remembered that she was still mad at him. Fair enough.

The couple signed the papers, paid, and Eli led them to the bikes, had them choose helmets, and then gave them some instructions and a map to the biking trails. He watched the pair grin at each other as they walked the bikes out of the shop.

If he couldn't guess what stopped Whitney last night, he didn't know if it was the kind of something that would make her not want to go with him to visit his parents tonight. He pulled out his phone and texted her.

Are we still on for tonight?

I never miss the chance to throw a bucket of water on a potential family fire. ;)

Her response came quickly, and she was joking around with him. Both good signs.

I'm not sure a bucket will be enough. Want me to stop by the fire station and borrow some turnouts to shield you from the flames?

Nah. I'll just bring some marshmallows and roasting sticks. Come pick me up at the paper whenever you're ready.

It'll be close to 7 before I'm there. You'll be there that late?

When you've got an editorial staff made entirely of people still in school, 7 isn't late at all.

Eli had the shop closed up, the books finished, and the deposit ready by 6:45. He walked three buildings over, and stepped into the Gazette's building for the first time since he was in high school. Whitney didn't see him walk in, so he just stayed at the door for a few moments so he could watch her in action. She was crouched down next to a high school girl at a desk, discussing an article the girl wrote.

They finished, and Whitney said, "This one's looking great. How's that article about the businesses participating in Fall Market?"

"Not finished yet."

"No problem. Let me know when you're ready for me to look at it." A little louder, Whitney said, "Scott. What do you have for me?"

"I've finished the one about how the freeway construction project ending is affecting tourism numbers *and* the one about the service project the Swingin' Seniors are doing for the newborn babies."

"You are brilliant and amazing," Whitney said. "Are you ready for me to come check them out?"

"Yeah," Scott said, "but I think maybe you should check out our guest instead."

Eli smiled as Whitney spun from her crouch to a standing position, facing him. "What's this I hear about you checking me out?" he asked.

Whitney laughed, and turned back to Scott. "Just email them to me, and I'll get edits back to you later."

She said goodbye to both of her employees, then went to her desk and grabbed her blazer from the back of her chair. Eli noticed that the swan he'd made her from the napkin at Keetch's was sitting on her desk and it made him smile. It was something, at least.

"You ready?"

Whitney swung her jacket on, and then grabbed a balloon bouquet from behind the door he hadn't noticed. "Am now."

They walked down Main Street, back to where his car was parked behind Treanor's. Whitney held the balloons in the hand nearest him, so they couldn't walk close together. She wasn't so all-business as she was when they'd first started planning the decorations at Keetch's, but he had definitely been friend-zoned.

The closer they got to his parents' house, the more nervous

Eli got. He was a grown man. A grown man with a very successful business. How could his dad always make him feel like a punk kid who couldn't get his life together? It had been a long time since he'd been that kid. He pulled into his parents' driveway, then got out of the car and opened the door for Whitney.

She must've sensed his apprehension, because she reached out, put her hand on his arm, and said, "You've got this."

He just gave her a smile that he didn't feel at all, and then went to the door. His mom smiled so big when she opened the door that Eli wondered if she was happier to see Whitney than she was to see him. His dad's face even lit up when they walked into his bedroom, where he was propped up in his bed with half a dozen pillows.

The conversation between him, Whitney, and his parents went smoothly. They talked about the paper, things going on in town, the weather, and tourism numbers. Bringing Whitney was a great idea. Maybe he could convince her to come with him every time.

"Let's see your shirt, dear," Eli's mom said, so Whitney pulled her blazer open a bit, and his mom read out loud, "'I'm a journalist; assume I'm write.' Oh that's funny. I haven't seen that one before. Did you see that, Robert? Instead of 'right,' it used 'write,' like writing an article."

His dad chuckled, and then adjusted himself in the bed, sucking in a pained breath.

"Oh, it's probably time for your medicine," Eli's mom said. "Let me get you some water."

"I'll get it," Whitney said. "You stay right here and rest— you look exhausted. Were you able to sleep at the hospital?" When Eli's mom nodded, Whitney added, "You probably didn't get much sleep, though. I'll be right back."

Eli stood when Whitney did. "I'll help."

Except when they got to the kitchen, Whitney didn't seem to need much help at all. "Your parents have had some rough days, and probably have some pretty rough ones ahead of them." She opened a cupboard and pulled out two glasses. "I should bring them dinner. Actually, I should go to the Helping Hands group at church, and see if we can get volunteers to bring them in dinner for the next week or so." She opened the fridge, pulled out a pitcher of water, and poured it into both cups. Then she opened a pantry door and pulled out a flat tray and put both cups of water on it. "These are probably his pills," she said, picking two bottles up from the counter.

"How do you know where everything is in their kitchen even better than I do?"

Whitney shrugged. "Because I lived here."

"You... What?" Eli stared at her, dazed.

"Well, I didn't *live here* live here." She put the medicine bottles on the tray. "Instead of going to University of Denver with me, like a good little sister, Jackie decided to go to University of South Carolina. A month into my senior year, my mom decided to join her there. I still came back home every weekend, though, because I still worked for the paper, but I no longer had a home to go to. So your parents and a couple other families took turns letting me stay with them."

Why had it not occurred to him to ask her about her family yet? Whitney studied his face for a moment, and must've figured out part of what he was feeling better than he figured out himself, because then she added, "Oh— you're jealous!"

Eli scoffed. "I'm not jealous. I went away by my own choice. Neither of them kicked me out. Plus, they weren't exactly together when I moved out."

"It's not like I moved in or anything, and it wasn't immediately— it was three years after you'd left. I drove into town on Saturday mornings, worked all day, hung out with friends in the evening, then came here late Saturday night, and packed my stuff back in my car Sunday morning and headed back to college right after church. And it was only once every three weeks." After a beat, she picked up the tray. "I think it helped them, having me here sometimes. It was like—" She crinkled her brow, like she was trying to figure out what she was trying to say. "Like a piece of you was here."

He let that news settle in as they walked back to his parents room and his dad took his medicine.

"So, son," his dad croaked, then cleared his throat a couple of times. "How's Treanor's doing?"

Eli knew from having his own business that if he were asking for an update when he had to be away, he'd want specifics, so that's what he'd prepared to give his dad. "The shop was busy almost constantly all weekend. I compared the numbers with two weekends ago, before they finished the construction on the freeway, and this weekend was up thirty percent. Today we had eighty percent of all summer rentals out at one point."

His dad raised an eyebrow, impressed. It was gone in an instant, though. "You didn't turn customers away because they didn't get there before the time on the doors said we were closing, right?"

A buzzing sounded, and Whitney picked up her phone. "It's my mom. I better take this, or she'll assume I'm dead or being held hostage and alert the National Guard."

Eli sighed as he watched her walk out of the room, and then turned back to his dad. "Don't worry— I waited until the last person who possibly wanted to come into the store got helped before I closed up the shop."

"What about the books? Did you do the books? You might be able to put off your books at your business for a week or even a month, but it's important to do the books every single day at Treanor's."

"I've done them daily, Dad. And I've dropped off the deposit daily. I found your home email address listed in the contacts for the business one, and I've been emailing you the daily totals on everything. So once you're feeling better, if you get curious about how things are, you can just log in."

"That's very thoughtful of you, honey," his mom said, patting his arm.

Eli didn't admit that he wasn't doing it to be thoughtful—he was doing it so that his dad didn't feel the need to hobble down to the shop in his bathrobe and scooter to see the numbers.

"You didn't copy and paste straight from the accounting software, right? Because there's account numbers in there, and email can be hacked."

"No account numbers, Dad."

Eli could tell by the muffled sounds coming from the other parts of the house that Whitney had been wandering as she spoke with her mom. He turned his head a bit as she wandered nearer so his ear was aimed her direction. Not that he was trying to hear what she was saying. His parents had noticed the shift, though, and their eyes went the direction Whitney was.

The expression on his dad's face immediately softened. "It's nice to see the two of you together again."

"We're not—"

"Together in the same place at the same time," he clarified.

His mom opened her mouth to speak, but paused, like she

hadn't quite figured out what to say. Finally, she said, "Be careful."

Eli's forehead crinkled and he cocked his head to the side. Seeing his confusion at her words, his mom exhaled and said, "When you left before, it was every bit as hard on her as it was on us. You'll be leaving again before too long, so just... be careful."

His dad coughed several times, and his mom put her hand on his arm in comfort. She handed him his water, and after taking a sip and clearing his throat, he said, "You might be okay with breaking hearts all over Sacramento, but you be careful with our Whitney's."

"Okay. Okay. Goodbye Mom. I love you, too." Whitney ended the call and slid the phone into her pocket as she walked into the room,

"How is your mom?" Eli's mom asked. "Did you have a good call?"

"She's doing well. The phone call was a bunch of 'are you eating healthy, how's the paper, why aren't you dating, when are you going to move to South Carolina with me and your sister'— the weekly usual."

"You're moving to South Carolina?" Eli asked, alarmed.

She laughed a quick bark of a laugh. "No. But it doesn't stop her from asking every phone call. I think she and my sister feel guilty for leaving me here. My roots here are too deep, though. I mean you could pull me up and transport me across the country, but I'm not sure these roots would survive outside of Nestled Hollow soil."

Even just sitting here, talking about mundane things in a room with poor lighting and 1980's decor, Whitney looked beautiful and radiant and had a happy calmness surrounding her. Eli knew that her heart wasn't the only one he needed to be careful with.

Chapter Eleven

*I*t was the time of the day when Whitney had finished being out in the town interviewing people or researching stories, and she was back at the office, about to write up her own articles. The time of the day when her college student and high school student staff (along with Lincoln, her once-a-week elementary school honorary staff member) were just getting out of school and would be in to work before too long. The time of the day when she was in the office alone, and if someone hadn't already texted her, she would go through her long list of people in town and find someone somewhere doing something. This town was her family, and they invited her to join with their families as readily as they invited their official family members.

She kept looking down at the list of people in town. These were the people she loved hanging out with— if she had her way, she'd hang out with all of them every night. A nightly town party. She really wanted to get together with people and socialize tonight. Yet when she looked at the list, she didn't feel compelled to call anyone. After a while of turning her phone over and over in her hand, she realized it was because she didn't want to hang out with *people;* she wanted to hang out with a *person.* A very specific person.

But that was a bad idea. A very bad idea. She needed to protect herself. She was a pro at protecting herself— some might even say that she was at master level. But even with all her experience, Eli had almost found a way inside her defenses up in the mountains. And that scared her more than she was willing to admit.

Yet she was so drawn to him. Probably because they had once been such good friends. Just because they were grown-ups now didn't mean they couldn't be friends like before. She could hang out with him as a friend. That was doable, she was sure of it.

After almost touching his phone number in her contacts, then turning off her phone, then almost touching his phone number, then turning off her phone, Whitney opened a text to Eli.

WOULD YOU LIKE TO GO HANG OUT SOMEWHERE TONIGHT?

No, that was way too bold, and made it sound like she was asking him on a date, which she very much was not doing.

OUR FALL MARKET PLANS ARE MISSING SOMETHING. CAN YOU MEET TO DISCUSS?

Perfect. No hidden messages there. She pushed send. It only took a few seconds before she saw the indicator that he was typing a response. She held her breath as the three dots kept moving back and forth.

She waited, staring at her screen. The screen darkened, so

she touched it to bring it back to life, and still the dots moved. Maybe he was struggling with figuring out how to tell her that he wasn't interested. Or that he already had plans. Or maybe he couldn't figure out whether he wanted to see her or not. Maybe she should've suggested they join another group of people, instead of implying that they were going to do something alone. Right before it went dark the second time, the indicator disappeared, as if he wasn't responding at all.

She turned off her phone and pushed it to the very edge of her desk. She wasn't in high school anymore, and her life didn't revolve around whether or not a boy could hang out with her tonight. She opened her word processor and typed *Service Spotlight of the Week*, pressed enter and typed *by Whitney Brennan*, then pressed enter again and stared at the flashing cursor.

And stared some more.

Then reminded herself that this was stupid, and to get to work. So she did. Two paragraphs into her article, her phone buzzed, and she nearly knocked over her water bottle trying to grab it.

Sorry. Customer came in while I was typing. Was going to try out some new waterproof lights on a canoe at sunset. Want to join me? I hear brainstorming is more effective when you're on a lake. I'm pretty sure there's scientific proof.

Whitney smiled as she typed in her response.

Then we should definitely test that theory. I'll meet you at the lake at 6.

Whitney drove through the tree-lined streets where the gold and red leaves were just beginning to fall. Before long, there would be enough on the ground up in the mountains that they could collect them for the Fall Market.

When she pulled into the parking area next to the lake, Eli was already at the shore, crouched down next to a canoe, working on something with his hands. She got out of the car, opened the back door, grabbed her jacket, and put it on. The sun wouldn't set for at least another twenty minutes, and it wouldn't be all the way dark for a good thirty minutes after that. But right now, the sun shone a golden light down on Eli, and if he needed any images for advertising or promotion— or even to hang up in his store, this was it.

She grabbed her bags, slung them over her neck, pulled her camera out, and headed down the incline. Eli was so engrossed in his work that he didn't see her coming. She stopped and got a few candid shots, then moved closer and to the side a bit and got a few more with the light at a different angle. She clicked through the shots, seeing if the settings needed to be adjusted. The pictures were amazing. Maybe she'd have to write a story for the paper about the lake or Treanor's Outdoor Recreation just to use them.

It wasn't until she got closer and stepped onto the gravelly area that Eli heard the crunch of her steps and turned to see her, his face lighting up in the evening sun. She put the camera to her eye and got a shot before his expression changed.

"I didn't realize this was going to be a photo shoot," Eli said.

Whitney lifted a shoulder in a shrug. "Impromptu. I couldn't resist this lighting."

Eli raised an eyebrow.

"Okay, okay, the subject matter was looking pretty great, too." She motioned at the set of lights he was attaching to the canoe. "So are you planning to start doing nighttime rentals?"

He shook his head. "My dad rarely rents at night, and if he does, it's only to people who really know what they're doing, and who are willing to sign that they won't even think about drinking, using drugs, or taking prescription medications that warn you against operating heavy machinery, and that they won't get within five feet of the water without a life jacket."

"A little riskier then, huh?"

"Only if you don't know what you're doing, make stupid choices, or go alone." He grinned up at her. "Thanks for coming."

"What are friends for, if not to keep you from making stupid choices?"

Eli laughed. "Yep— that's exactly why I asked you to come with me." He'd said it sarcastically, which made Whitney smile.

Once Eli was finished preparing the canoe, he tossed Whitney a life jacket, and put one on himself. She zipped her camera into its waterproof bag and secured it under one of the seats. Then she climbed in the front seat while Eli pushed the boat into the water and hopped in himself. The canoe rocked back and forth a bit before steadying itself. Eli pulled the oars from the bottom of the canoe, and handed one to Whitney.

When they reached the middle of the lake, Whitney turned around in her seat so she was facing Eli, and slid the oar back into the bottom of the canoe. The sun was just beginning to set, and was throwing brilliant oranges and pinks across the sky, the pine trees and homes silhouetted against its brilliance. She bit her lip, wishing she dared to pull her camera out and chance it getting wet.

Eli must've been studying her expression pretty intently, because he said, "Go ahead. I'll make sure to keep the boat steady."

Whitney nodded, then pulled her camera out of its protective bag, and lined up the perfect shot. From out here, she even got the reflection of the sunset on the lake. She got a few shots, and then shifted the camera to the right a bit, catching a silhouette of Eli. She thought she was being sneaky, until he clapped his hands together above his head, framing his face, and she burst out laughing.

"How long has it been since you've been out here?" Eli asked as she put her camera away.

"Canoeing?" Whitney looked up. "Two weekends ago for the Relay for Restoration project." She turned her head and flashed him a grin. "My team won. How about you? How long has it been?"

"Much too long. I'd forgotten how incredible it feels to be out here. There's not a whole lot I wouldn't do to have a small lake like this at TeamUp. We could do so many activities on this lake." He gestured at the flat open space on the beach where the town gathered for celebrations and games. "We've got an area similar to that, only much bigger. All we need is a lake."

"TeamUp is your company?"

He nodded, and a smile filled his entire face, his body shifting in excitement. "I run it with a guy named Ben, who's my business partner and longtime friend. Businesses send us their employees for team building exercises. Sometimes it's as few as five people; sometimes it's as many as five hundred.

There's nothing quite like starting out with a group of people who can't even stand to look at each other, and have them laughing and getting along by the end."

Whitney smiled. "It sounds like maybe you two should be marriage counselors."

Eli chuckled. "We've done a few groups where everyone brought their spouses, and we've done partner building activities."

"Like what? Let's do one."

Eli glanced around, his hands out, like he was reaching for something that wasn't there. "I'm not sure there's a whole lot we can do in a canoe. I can't exactly have one of us lead the other on a blind walk, or go blindfolded through an obstacle course. Or lean into each other while walking. Or tie one of our hands behind our backs and try making a paper airplane together using just one arm from each of us. I don't even think I'd dare have us sit back to back in here and try to stand up. We'd probably find ourselves swimming in the lake. Oh! I've got it."

He tugged out a bag he'd pushed under his seat, unzipped it, and pulled out an electric lantern. After carefully placing it on the floor of the canoe between them, he turned it on, bathing them in light.

"Okay, in this activity, we have to look in each other's eyes for ninety seconds without talking."

Whitney looked to the left and then the right, waiting for him to give more information, but he didn't. "Okay," she dragged the word out, "and do what?"

"Nothing. Just look."

"Without blinking?"

He shook his head. "You can blink."

"Do you have to keep a straight face? If you make the other person crack a smile, do you win?"

"You can smile. This isn't a contest, Whitney— this is to get both people on the same team."

"How is that a partner building activity?"

"When was the last time you met someone's eyes for a full ninety seconds?"

Whitney shrugged. "Probably all the time."

An amused smile played on Eli's face. Whitney decided it was one of her favorite looks on him. "It's different than you think. A full ninety seconds, and you can't look away."

She could see the challenge in his expression, like maybe it was going to be more difficult than she thought. She was ready to take on that challenge. There was a reason her team always won everything. "Bring it on."

Eli pulled his phone out of his pocket, held down the button, and said, "Set timer for ninety seconds."

Whitney smiled and raised an eyebrow, the only way she could think of to smack talk without actually talking. Eli smiled back. Goodness, he had a beautiful smile. She wondered if he realized how beautiful it was. Probably. She made a few faces at him, and was rewarded with a soft chuckle.

She tried to keep her face impassive, but she was suddenly self-conscious with all of his attention so hyper-focused on her. She nearly looked down and couldn't believe that she was so close to almost losing! *Focus*, she told herself.

He was looking at her so intently, though, that she stopped making silly faces and just looked at him as fiercely as he was looking at her. His eyes were even more incredible than she had remembered. Dark lashes framed the most brilliant blue eyes. She'd always thought of them as being ice blue, but now that she was really looking, she noticed that they were light blue and like the most exquisite gems close to his pupils, but were also ringed with a blue so deep, like the night sky moments before the first hints of dawn peeked in. The light from the lantern reflected off his eyes, making it look like stars in that night sky. She could get lost in those eyes.

Those eyes that seemed to be able to see into her soul. Could he tell what she was thinking? It looked like he could. Actually, it looked like he could see past what she was thinking, right down to what she was feeling. Like maybe he could see even further— to the parts of her that she hadn't even figured out about herself.

How long was ninety seconds, anyway? Shouldn't his alarm have gone off by now?

She wondered if she could see the same in him if she just looked hard enough. As the waves lapped against the sides of the canoe, rocking them gently, she focused on those eyes, on everything those eyes were expressing. A longing. A sadness. A calm contentedness. Joy. Could they be showing joy and sadness at the same time? Maybe so. At least that's what she guessed his eyes were showing. She wasn't very good at this— clearly not as good at it as he was, or she'd have a look of confidence on her face like he did.

Maybe he just knew what he wanted out of life. He'd obviously found a job that made him deliriously happy with a business partner he couldn't talk about without a note of respect in his voice. And now he had to be away from that to be somewhere he didn't choose to be. She wondered if his being back in Nestled Hollow was as confusing to him as it was to her. Because before he'd shown up out of the blue, if anyone would've asked her if she'd have had any interest in spending time with Eli again, she would've given an emphatic no. But now, with him back, she was every bit as drawn to him as she'd been back in high school.

And now he was even more *Eli* than he'd been back then. If she was being honest with herself, she wasn't finding ways to spend time with him because he was a good friend. She was finding ways to spend time with him because she was possibly even more in love with him now than she'd been back in high school. She gasped, covering her mouth with both hands. She was still in love with him? How had she not seen that coming?

Eli's phone let out a buzzing tune, and he touched the stop button.

"Whoa," Whitney said. "That was.... Whoa."

Chapter Twelve

hitney's reaction to the partner building activity made him smile. He hadn't ever done the activity himself, and was just as blown away as she was. Had he really been comparing every woman he'd ever dated to Whitney? And in those early years, when he'd first started dating again, had he really been purposely choosing only toxic, damaging relationships that were doomed from the start, just to stay available for her?

The exercise left him more confused than ever. How could he be so very interested in someone in Nestled Hollow when he loved the life he had in Sacramento? The two couldn't co-exist. TeamUp was the thing that helped him to figure out who he was and what he wanted in life. But being with Whitney here made him realize what it was that he'd been missing in Sacramento. Whitney's roots were deep here, though. He couldn't have both.

"I've got the next partner activity," Whitney said, startling him out of his thoughts.

"Really."

"Really," she said, pulling the second bag from under her seat and feeling around inside. With a flourish, she lifted out something wrapped in paper. "I stopped at Joey's Pizza and Subs on my way here. Is roast beef with everything still your favorite?"

"Oh," he said, a pained expression on his face. "I forgot to tell you. I'm vegan now."

"You are not," she said, smacking him in the arm, causing the canoe to rock back and forth, before putting the sandwich in his lap and pulling out a second one for herself.

She opened her sandwich, and just before she took her first bite, he said, "Wait," and she paused, sandwich halfway to her open mouth. "This is not the appropriate lighting for Joey's Pizza and Subs." He turned off the lantern, and before his eyes could adjust to the moonlight, they were plunged into momentary darkness. He felt for the switch to the lights he'd installed just under the outside ridge of the canoe and flipped them on.

Light glowed all around the canoe and danced across the waves, bouncing on the water more than a dozen feet away. He took out his cell phone and snapped a picture of the wonder crossing Whitney's face as she gazed across the lake in amazement.

"Eli," she breathed as she looked around, mesmerized. "This is the most incredible thing I've ever seen."

"Thank you, thank you. I'll be here all season." He'd known it was the wrong thing to say the moment he said it, even before Whitney's gaze dropped to her lap. In an effort to get back the lightness from before, he grasped for anything to talk about. "So, do you talk to your mom often?" *Nice. You're on a beautiful lake in the moonlight with an amazing woman, and you ask about her mom.*

"About once a week. I go visit her and my sister every

summer, and they come visit me every Christmas. South Carolina is absolutely beautiful and every time I go there, they try to talk me into moving, and I'm tempted. I mean, they've got the ocean practically in their backyard. Then when they come here, they're reminded of how beautiful Nestled Hollow is, and they're tempted to move back. After all, we've got these mountains and this lake."

"And Joey's Pizza and Subs," Eli said, holding his up as evidence.

Whitney laughed. "That almost tips the scales for here, of course. But the truth is, South Carolina is perfect for them and Nestled Hollow is perfect for me, and none of us are really going to ever move."

What was Eli thinking? Why was he torturing himself by getting closer to Whitney? It could never work out, so it was just going to make Ben get his wish— he'd go back home brokenhearted. He just needed to focus on the decorations for Fall Market when he was around her. Get that done and over with, then focus on his dad's business and TeamUp.

"Scavenger hunt," he blurted out.

Whitney had just taken a bite, and gave him a confused look. She chewed quickly, swallowed, and then said, "What?"

"For Fall Market. We should have a scavenger hunt, and have things that people have to find that take them into different businesses and booths along Main Street." By the look on Whitney's face, she'd completely forgotten the reason they'd met up in the first place. He forged on, making sure the conversation turned its way to where it should be. "It would be good for businesses, and it would be a fun activity for the shoppers. Maybe we could get some donations for good prizes to really encourage people to play."

"Yeah, that sounds really great. I bet all the businesses

would be on board with that. We should bring it up at the Business Alliance meeting on Thursday, and get a list of who wants to participate, and get them thinking about what to have people search for in their stores, and if they can donate."

Eli nodded. "I think setting up the decorations is going to be tough, and will probably take a while. How long will we have to prepare?"

"I can get half the town to come help. With enough people working together, I don't think it'll take too long. We should probably start gathering stuff, though. I can start calling people in town who use wood burning stoves, and see if they have some logs cut up that we can turn on their end to use as seats around the campfires."

Eli tried not to flinch when he said, "I'll ask my dad if we can borrow his truck to go pick them up. We can just line them along the side of Treanor's. It might even start getting people excited."

"And we'll go get leaves this weekend?"

"Sounds good," Eli said.

See? He could keep this relationship focused on what it was— a partnership to plan a town event. Nothing more.

Piece of cake.

He finished his sandwich, wadded the wrapper into a ball and tossed it into his bag. "We better get heading back," he said, and picked up an oar and started paddling back to shore.

Eli was proud of himself. He didn't have any Fall Market things to discuss, so he didn't text Whitney once on Wednesday. He couldn't say that he hadn't thought about her all day, or looked at the picture he'd taken of her when she saw the canoe's lights on the water, or thought about everything that had gone through his mind as he'd looked in her eyes for ninety seconds, but not texting her felt like progress. Like maybe he could survive this interruption to his regular life with minimal heartbreak.

Thursday morning, he got a text from Whitney, asking if they could head straight from the Business Alliance meeting to the Willard home, because they might have all the logs they needed. Still Fall Market-related. That felt safe. He called his dad, asked to borrow his truck, and endured all the "You aren't going to leave the shop not staffed well enough while it's open, right?" and "Do you promise not to hot rod in my truck?" questions, and went and picked up the truck, thankfully while his dad was taking a nap, and drove it to the meeting.

He was doing pretty well at the meeting, too. He sat at the back, right behind the tallest person he could find in the crowd, blocking Whitney from his view. Then, of course, Linda Keetch asked the two of them to come to the front and update everyone on how the decorations were coming.

Whitney started telling about what they had planned. She was so at home in front of the group, and excitement about the event was coming off her in waves. It made him excited for it all over again. They both jumped in, telling one part after another, like a dance they both knew their parts to perfectly. The Business Alliance got excited, too, and was on board with everything.

By the time they left the meeting, they were both breathless, like they'd just run a race.

"It's going to turn out as well as we're imagining, right?" Whitney asked as she climbed into the passenger's side of his dad's truck.

"Of course it will."

They drove to the Willard home, loaded up twenty-seven logs, each of them about twenty inches tall and big around enough for an adult to sit on, and drove all the way back to Treanor's Outdoor Rentals, all while keeping the subject of conversation on the Fall Market. If this was a contest with himself, Eli was winning.

Since Treanor's was on the corner, he was able to pull the truck right up to the side of the building, so they wouldn't have to walk far with the logs. They had only unloaded half a dozen when a kid came along on a bike. He parked it on the sidewalk, and Whitney said, "Hey, Lincoln! I had to leave the office a bit early today. Did you drop off your article while I was gone?"

The little kid grinned. "Of course. A junior reporter always meets his deadlines." Then he saluted Whitney, and she saluted back. Then they did some kind of fist bump sequence that Eli hadn't ever seen before. Then he asked her to stand up straight so he could read her shirt. "I'm very FONT of you—you're just my TYPE." He looked like he didn't quite get it, but didn't ask for an explanation. "I think I like your one that says 'Newspaper journalist— only because full time multitasking ninja isn't an actual job title' better." After looking around, he said, "So, whatcha doin'?"

"Hauling logs," Eli said. "Do you want to help?"

The kid couldn't have been more than eight or nine, but his face lit up. Eli tossed him a pair of gloves, and hoped the logs weren't too heavy for the kid to lift. He suggested that they do it assembly-line style. Eli grabbed a log from the back of the truck, and then handed it to Lincoln. If it was heavy and the kid looked like he was struggling, Whitney could grab it from him before he even had to take a step.

"Wow, look at those muscles," Eli said when Lincoln passed along the first log.

"We're going to get done in no time with this extra help," Whitney added.

They passed several along that way, until Lincoln looked like he was starting to get tired. Then Eli said, "You guys must be machines, because I'm beat. Do you mind taking a break for a minute so I can rest?" Then he went to the cab of the truck, pulled out a six pack of water bottles, and tossed one to Whitney and one to Lincoln before opening one himself.

As they all leaned against the side of the truck, drinking their water, he felt Whitney's eyes on him. He turned to look at her, and tried to figure out what the look on her face was. "What?"

Whitney shook her head, like she hadn't realized she'd been staring. She paused for a minute, gloves hanging out of the pockets of her jeans, running her finger along the top of the water bottle. "Do you ever think about having kids?"

"Yeah," Eli said. "Of course. I've always wanted kids. Not just one, like my parents did, but a whole houseful of kids. I just—" He didn't know how to finish the sentence, so he let it trail off. But Whitney kept looking at him, expecting him to finish. He took a breath and then just dumped it out, without letting himself think if it was a good idea first. "I've just got too many flaws to even get to the husband part, let alone the dad part."

Whitney opened her mouth, like she was about to say something, but no words came out. Her forehead crinkled in confusion. Instead of letting her dwell on whatever she was thinking about him, he asked, "What about you?"

"Same," she said, her voice barely coming out in a whisper.

He looked at her with the same bewilderment she was

looking at him with. And for the smallest moment, he wondered if that dream of a wife and a houseful of kids was actually possible. He allowed himself to picture it as he and Whitney locked eyes. He allowed himself to picture living here in Nestled Hollow, and he was surprised to realize how much he'd like that.

Lincoln screwed the lid on his water bottle, plunked it down on the side of the truck, and said, "So are you two going to just stare at each other all day, or are we going to finish unloading this wood?"

Chapter Thirteen

*A*lthough they had texted quite a bit throughout yesterday, Whitney hadn't seen Eli at all. Somehow not seeing him made her look forward to their trip up the mountain even more. The weather had turned colder over the past couple of days, so she dressed for the change. She didn't go into the paper on Saturdays, so she didn't feel the need to wear her usual "uniform." Instead, she put on a favorite pair of jeans, brown knee high boots, a long sleeved t-shirt, and her red coat.

She took one last look in her full-length mirror, fluffed her hair a bit, and rearranged a curl. She looked ready to head up into the mountains with a ridiculously handsome man and collect leaves.

Pausing at her front door, Whitney turned to look at her empty apartment. She took a moment and thought back to when she'd been working with Eli to unload the logs on Thursday evening, and pictured what she'd pictured then: her kitchen and living room filled with Eli and a bunch of kids. The thought was just as thrilling— and scary and impossible

—as it had been then. She headed out to her car and drove to Treanor's, pulling into the lot behind the store.

Eli was already in the parking lot next to a four wheeler, hooking a trailer up to it that was at least twice as long as the all-terrain vehicle itself. Just like he'd promised, the trailer was packed with boxes that they could load up with the fall leaves. He finished whatever he was doing with the hitch, stood up straight, and gave her one of his crooked smiles, and she let out a breathless sigh.

"You ready to head up?"

Whitney nodded, and hefted her bag of water bottles into the trailer with the boxes. Eli put on a helmet, handed one to her, then slung a leg over the seat of the four-wheeler and started it up.

Whitney stepped on the foot rest, and then slung her other leg over the seat, too. She was sitting with her legs up against his, her hands out at her sides, and suddenly she didn't know what to do with them. In all her preparations for heading up into the mountains with Eli, she hadn't actually thought about this part. Many times over the past week and a half, Eli had felt like her old best friend. And if that's where they still were, she'd have wrapped her arms around his stomach and held on tight without thinking anything of it. Now, though, things felt different, and she didn't quite know what to do.

The four-wheeler gave a lurch as he eased it forward, and she threw her arms around his stomach. His muscles tightened as soon as her hands were on them, and she smiled. At least she wasn't the only one who noticed that this just felt different.

As they drove past Main Street, several people on the sidewalks turned at the sound of the four-wheeler and waved.

They both waved back. John Erickson called out, motioning to the trailer, "Is this something to do with Fall Market?"

"It sure is!" Eli called back.

"I can't wait to see what you do."

Whitney smiled. Eli seemed to slowly be coming around to accepting that the town did actually like him. He'd been so quick to join in a crowd when he'd lived here before, but she'd noticed that he held back most of the time when it came to people in town. It was nice to see him opening up a bit.

It didn't take long before they reached the spot where the paved road from town gave way to the dirt road that led up the mountainside. As the road got steeper and steeper, Whitney had to adjust her hold on Eli so she wouldn't slide off the back of the four-wheeler. As soon as her hands were on his chest, heat rushed to her face, and she laid her head against his back to hide her blush. Which was stupid, because it wasn't like he could see her blush anyway, and now she also had her cheek against his back. So maybe it wasn't a stupid decision after all, because his back felt amazing, and he smelled amazing. She closed her eyes and basked in the scent of his freshly laundered shirt, mixing with the pine and sunshine smells of the mountains, feeling the shift of his back muscles as he steered the vehicle up the rocky road.

The road up the mountain was much windier than the path of the ski tram, so the trip took much longer. She wasn't complaining. When they reached the flat area at the top of the ski lift, Eli parked the four wheeler, the back end of the trailer near the trail they'd taken the time they'd come up last week.

She slid off the ATV first, and then Eli switched the engine off and got off as well. After taking off her helmet and placing it on the seat, she tried to fix what she was sure was a crazy new hairstyle. Eli took his helmet off, too, and ran a hand through his curls. She didn't realize she'd frozen in mid-hair-fixing, staring at him, until he said, "What?"

Whitney leaned in closer to him, making a show of inspecting him. "Just checking for bug splatters. You didn't have the same wind shield that I had."

Eli smiled big, showing all his teeth. Whitney inspected those, too. She wiped a pretend bug off his cheek and said, "Lookin' good."

"Thank you for your service," Eli said.

Whitney pulled on some thin gardening gloves, and they each grabbed a box and a leaf rake and headed up the path to the clearing surrounded by trees with fall leaves that they'd found last time. The area was covered in easily five times the number of leaves that they'd seen a week ago. They started raking the leaves into piles, then scooping them up by the armful and putting them into the boxes.

"So you worked at the Nestled Hollow Gazette through high school and college. What happened after college?"

"I came back here and worked part time at the Nestled Hollow Gazette, and wrote freelance articles for half a dozen other newspapers until Mr. Annesley asked me if I could start working full time so that he could take a step back, and he started slowly turning more and more responsibilities over to me. Three years ago, he said he wanted me to run the paper when he retired, and that he was signing the deed over to me. Everyone thought he'd never retire."

"I remember him loving the paper. And he did kind of seem like the type of person who would work until he died."

Whitney got a little choked up. "Yeah, well, he had decided to retire— that very weekend— which totally caught me off guard. I still had so much to learn. Running the paper is a bit of a different responsibility than owning it. But he said he'd be around forever, so I could ask all the questions I wanted. But the weekend he retired, he left for a retirement trip to the coast. He never made it. He got in a massive car accident on the way." Emotions welled up inside her, working their way up until her last sentence had barely come out as a whisper.

She cleared her throat and wiped away a stray tear. "I don't actually talk about Mr. Annesley. New subject. Um..." She racked her brain, trying to think of anything she could ask Eli that would get him to open up about his past, but trying to push down all the past emotions about Mr. Annesley made her brain foggy and she couldn't think of any. So she said, "Tell me something I don't know."

In an obvious effort to help pull her out of the dark place her emotions had gone, Eli said, "Sixteen point four million American adults believe that chocolate milk comes from brown cows."

A laugh burst out of Whitney, and she wiped a stray tear with the back of her glove and grabbed another armful of leaves.

"When you spell out odd numbers, every single one of them has the letter E in it." After a pause, he added, "Movie trailers used to be shown after the movie. That's why they're called 'trailers.' And did you know that rats and chimpanzees are the only animals that can legitimately find something humorous and laugh?"

Whitney laughed, rolled her eyes, and then gave him a pointed look.

"Oh!" Eli said, feigning innocence. "You wanted me to tell you something you don't know about *me*."

He raked another section of the leaves into a pile, biting his lip. Then he stood the rake up straight, leaning against it, and he looked so perfect she wished her camera was still around her neck so she could snap a picture. "I've got one. So we were best friends for a long time, right?"

Whitney nodded. "Since a week before junior year."

"But we didn't start dating until four months before the end of our senior year."

Whitney nodded again. In truth, she'd been in love with him since the end of her sophomore year— since before they'd even become friends. They'd been in several classes together, and she'd seen the way he interacted with both people he was friends with and the people he was just acquaintances with, watching to see if he acted differently depending on who he was around. He didn't. He seemed to accept everyone as they were, with no judgement, and always reached out to anyone who was alone. It had been what had drawn her to him the most.

She'd just been one of his acquaintances back then. It wasn't until after her dad died, and he came to the lake one day while she was skipping rocks that they became friends. He hadn't seemed interested in being more than friends, but being friends with Eli Treanor soon became one of the most important things in her life.

Eli laid down his rake, scooped up an armful of leaves, and dropped them into the box she was filling, crouched down just across the box from her. "I was in love with you from the beginning. From that day at the lake a week before eleventh grade."

Whitney's head whipped up. "You were?"

Eli grabbed another armful of leaves and dropped them into the box. "I saw the way you drew people in, made them feel a part of something bigger than themselves. You helped them feel like they belonged. People shone around you—they always have. And then that day at the lake, seeing you struggle when you had helped so many others who were struggling and I don't know. There was something about that moment that made me know I loved you and that I always would."

He picked up a few leaves that hadn't made it into the box. "I could tell that you wanted to keep it at friendship, though. I wanted any kind of relationship with you that you were willing to give, so I never let you know I was in love with you. Then, four months before graduation, things were getting worse with my dad, and for the first time during my parents' separation, things with my mom got bad. I was pretty bummed, so you took me to the park. Do you remember that?"

Whitney nodded. "We swung on the swings for what felt like hours, just talking. I had been stressed about end-of-term school projects and preparing for college and graduation coming up— all things that my dad had promised to help me with, and I was feeling the sting of his death all over again. So I unloaded on you."

"I think we lifted the weight off each other's shoulders that night."

Whitney let out a quiet laugh. "And then we took those weights and chucked them as far as we could. I hadn't felt so light and carefree for months. Maybe years."

"You said we should watch a make-it-up-as-you-go movie, and you even popped popcorn. You spread a blanket on the grass right in the middle of Snowdrift Springs Park, and we lay on our backs, staring up at the stars, making up our own constellations. And then combining them to tell the story of Petey the one-legged kid who got in a hot air balloon and flew to the land of the bird people, where he dropped fluffy pieces of cotton candy down to them, because he felt bad that they didn't have any arms when he had two."

"And they had to catch the cotton candy in their mouths

because they didn't have any hands to catch it with!" Whitney smiled, remembering the story she hadn't thought about in so long.

Eli stood and picked up the rake, raking the last section of leaves into a pile. "And then we threw popcorn up into the air, trying to make it land in the other person's mouth, like it was cotton candy coming down from the sky."

Whitney laughed out loud. "I'm pretty sure I won that challenge."

"Only if you consider 'winning' as 'being the person with the most popcorn kernels stuck in their hair by the end.'"

"Oh, come on. I was the better aim."

"As you claimed that night. All I can say is I was still getting popcorn salt out of my eyes for days."

Whitney laughed as she scooped up more leaves, and longed for that time when they'd been such great friends.

"Then there was a moment where you looked at me and I looked at you and I think some actual electricity sparked between us— I know I was practically blinded— and we both went in for a kiss at the same time."

"That was a pretty glorious kiss."

Eli nodded. "It was. I knew right at that moment that I should probably apologize for the kiss. To say it was a mistake and reaffirm that we were just friends. But when I opened my mouth to say that, 'Will you go to prom with me?' came out instead." He stopped raking and met her eyes. "Do you wish I would've just apologized for the kiss instead?"

She'd thought he wasn't going to leave for college until the same time she was— at the end of the summer after senior year. In fact, a big part of their plans had them both going to the University of Denver together. She'd been so afraid back then that if they started dating, that it would ruin their friendship. And their friendship was such a huge part of her life that she couldn't bear the thought of anything happening to it. But she'd often wondered if she'd have opened herself to the possibility of dating sooner if she'd have known he'd be gone by the end of graduation night.

Then of course, if they had started dating sooner, it probably would've made everything worse. Coping with him leaving when he'd been both her best friend and her boyfriend of four months was almost too much to bear. Having to deal with him leaving when he'd been her boyfriend for longer might've been more than she could handle.

"I don't know," she said truthfully. "It probably would've made things easier if you had. Although I do remember a few other knee-buckling kisses we shared. It would've been a shame to miss out on those."

Eli grinned, and together, they scooped up the last of the leaves and put them into boxes.

Chapter Fourteen

*E*li couldn't take his eyes off Whitney as she straightened up, gloved hands on her hips, and looked around. The perfect silhouette against the fall colors, the golden sun making her face radiant, and she just stood there, seemingly oblivious to how beautiful she was. He cursed the eighteen-year-old Eli who had run away from this.

"We still have four empty boxes. If we don't fill them all, I doubt we'll have enough." She walked over to a maple tree whose branches reached out over the orchard. A breeze came by just then, blowing a sprinkling of leaves onto the ground. She looked up, studying the leaves that clung to the tree in masses. "These all look like they'll fall by tonight and it'd be more than enough. Where's a big strong gust of wind when you need it?"

"Allow me." Eli backed up to the other end of the clearing, and then took off running as fast as he could in the small area. Just before he reached Whitney, he jumped up and grabbed hold of a branch of the tree. He bounced his weight up and down while hanging from the branch, sending a cascade of leaves sprinkling down on Whitney.

A laugh burst out of her, echoing off the mountainside as thousands of leaves fluttered all around her. She put her arms out and twirled around in a circle, wonder and excitement coming off her in waves. Eli gave one last bounce on the branch, then let go and dropped to the ground. He joined Whitney, putting his arms around her waist and spinning around with her, leaves falling all around them. As they came to a stop, all the wonder and excitement that she'd been sending out toward the leaves was suddenly focused on him, and heat exploded in his chest.

Leaving one hand on her waist, he reached up and plucked a leaf from her hair, then ran his knuckles lightly down her neck. He looked at the way her deep, richly-colored auburn hair fell in soft curls, barely skimming her shoulders. He'd never seen anyone whose hair color so perfectly complemented her skin color. Especially when she blushed, like she was right now.

And those eyes! The brilliant green was the perfect contrast to her hair. Those eyes that accepted, that cared about everyone, that showed kindness and grace and a sense of humor. Those eyes studied his, and he felt like no matter what was wrong in his life, gazing into her eyes healed it all.

Whitney reached out and put a hand on his cheek, resting it there for a moment, before running her fingers down his neck, her hand coming to a rest on his chest, leaving a trail of electricity in its path. Her eyes shifted to his lips for a moment before coming back to his eyes.

He ran his knuckles along her jaw line, pausing at her chin and reaching out with a single finger to touch her lips. Her lips parted slightly, and he exhaled. He moved his hand to her back, sliding it down to match his other hand on her waist. Just as he was leaning in to her, she closed the distance and their lips met. Her lips were soft against his, moving slowly and carefully. She reached her hand up to his neck, running her fingers through his hair, causing his breath to catch and goose bumps to zing down his spine. He pulled her closer, their bodies touching, and suddenly his hands were cupped on the back of her head, his fingers tangled in her hair, as if he could hold this kiss in his hands. She pulled his head closer, and her kiss became fiercer, like she needed it as much as he did.

After a moment that seemed timeless yet over too soon, they broke the kiss and stood, foreheads touching, breathing in the same air.

Why had he been in such a hurry to leave all those years ago? He couldn't think of a single reason why just then. "I think I know now what's been missing from my life for the past twelve years."

Whitney let out a soft laugh as she ran her fingertips along his neck. "When I said our first kiss was glorious— well, let's just say that it had nothing on that one."

Eli walked into the chapel and glanced around, looking for the deep auburn of Whitney's hair. They hadn't planned to meet for church, but she was the type of person who went to church every week, so he figured he'd see her here. After yesterday in the mountains, he couldn't stop thinking about her. And he definitely couldn't go all day without seeing her.

"Eli!"

He turned when he heard his name, and saw his mother

walking toward him, her arms outstretched. As she neared, he reached out and gave her a hug. "What are you doing here, Mom? Is Dad home alone? Is it okay to leave him this soon?"

"It's been ten days since the surgery, and your father is doing pretty well. He said he could handle things on his own for a couple of hours so I could come get refueled." She leaned in and whispered conspiratorially, while patting her handbag, "I've got my cell phone in here, set to silent. I told him to text me if he has any issues, and I'll rush home, quick as a fox, to help him." She glanced around the rows and rows of pews. "Look! There's a couple of spots open next to Margie. Oh, it'll be so great to have my son next to me at church once again."

Eli spotted Whitney just then— of course, in the middle of a pew, surrounded by people. She turned his direction, meeting his eyes, and her face lit up. He gestured to his mom, who was walking up the aisle ahead of him, and gave an "I'm sorry, but I couldn't say no" shrug. She brought her hands together and gave an exaggerated "Aww, that's so cute!" face. Then she winked. He thought she was about to turn back to face the front, but at the last second, hesitated, her eyes still on his, and he could tell that she was thinking of their kiss. "See you after?" he mouthed. She smiled, gave a slight nod, and turned around.

Eli sat on the bench next to his mom, who had a smile spread from ear to ear. She re-introduced him to Margie, an older woman who looked exactly how Eli had remembered her— a face filled with the wrinkles you can only get from smiling at everyone you see, patting them on the cheek, and telling them how grown up they're looking. Margie smiled and reached across his mom and patted his knee. "It's so great to see you again, Eli. My, you've grown into a handsome man."

He smiled back. It was nice to know that some things stayed exactly the same.

When the gray-haired pastor from Eli's youth got up to deliver his sermon, Eli's mind had still been on Whitney. But the more the pastor spoke, the more he tuned in.

"How much of our energy is consumed by holding grudges, not letting go of feelings of anger, nursing old wounds, or remaining bitter? Forgiving others is not only vital to healthy relationships with others, but it's also vital to our own peace and growth as an individual."

He had left with nothing at all from his parents. It had been his choice to leave, true, but he'd always felt he was pushed away. That his parents especially had been the ones doing the pushing, and a part of him had been angry at them for it. He always thought that they should be seeking his forgiveness, since he was the one who was wronged. But now, hearing the pastor speak, he wondered if maybe he should be doing some forgiving regardless.

How much had his not forgiving held him back over the years? Maybe he could get all this figured out, and things would really work out between Whitney and him. When he walked out onto the lawn for the luncheon after church was over, and saw Whitney, talking to a group of people, her face lit up in happiness, he was sure that maybe things really could work out.

Chapter Fifteen

*W*hitney went from one group to another on the lawn of the church, saying hello to everyone. When someone hugged her from behind, wrapping her shoulders in a hug so enthusiastic it could only be one person, Whitney spun around and said to her friend Brooke, "You're back! How was L.A.?"

"Look at that," Brooke said. "You actually remember where your best friend went if you text her while she's gone. How is your hot man, anyway?"

Whitney looked around the crowd, searching for him. He stood next to his mom and a few other ladies in town. He met her gaze and smiled.

Brooke whirled around to face Whitney and gasped. "You kissed!"

Whitney shushed her friend. "We don't need to announce it to the entire congregation. And how can you always guess these things?"

Brooke lifted one shoulder in a shrug. "It's a gift. It also comes in handy when talking to a legendary designer at a swanky party in L.A."

"Did he agree to look at your portfolio?"

"He did."

"This is *huge*! I can't believe you didn't lead with that!"

"Honey, it's not nearly as huge as you actually dating again. And to top it off, kissing him." Brooke turned back in Eli's direction. Her words sounded normal for Brooke, but something about her was off.

"What aren't you telling me?" Whitney asked. "Did he agree to recommend you to some of his connections?"

Brooke lifted one shoulder in a shrug, and then shook her head. "Showing him my portfolio didn't actually go so well. There was a mix-up with his assistant, and then a miscommunication that turned out rather embarrassing for both of us, and," she winced, "a slight case of food poisoning that turned out pretty unfortunate."

"Oh, Brooke, I'm so sorry."

"So the only thing he was likely to pass along to his connections is a message blacklisting me."

Whitney hugged her friend tightly and said the words Brooke had said to her whenever she was feeling down. "It'll work out."

Brooke sniffed a few times, and then gave Whitney a tighter squeeze. "Things always do." She wiped away a tear, and then smiled.

"Do you want to go somewhere and talk?"

Brooke shook her head. "I've always said your hugs have magical healing powers—I'm feeling better already."

Whitney studied her for a moment, trying to see if Brooke was really okay, wishing she had Brooke's ability to know exactly how someone was feeling. And her ability to bounce back from disappointments.

"I'm *fine*," Brooke said. "Or at least I will be soon. Life has ups and downs and I just got to check one of the downs off my list. I'm fairly certain that means something good is in my near future." She nodded toward where Eli stood. "And speaking of goodness, Eli sure looks mighty fine in a suit. Didn't I say he would look mighty fine in a suit?"

Whitney kept her eyes on her friend for a few more moments, and then decided that either she was actually okay, or she didn't want to dwell on it. She would have to stop by the bakery and then take some late night cookies over to her apartment later to see how she was really doing.

Her gaze joined Brooke's, back to Eli, who was definitely looking mighty fine. His gray suit must've been tailored, because it fit his athletic body perfectly, showing off his strong shoulders and lean build. His curls were perfectly tamed for church, and his blue tie made his eyes stand out, even from this distance. He was talking with a group of his mother's friends, and just like when he was younger, everyone's attention was riveted to him, laughing, and having a good time. He didn't even seem to realize how adorable he was, and how much people were naturally drawn to him.

"I had no idea you had it this bad, girl."

Whitney's attention went back to Brooke. She hadn't realized that her friend had been watching her watch Eli, and she blushed. "Well, look at him!" She held both her arms out as evidence. "Look at the way his mom is beaming, just having him by her side, showing him off to her friends. How could you not find that adorable?"

Brooke nudged Whitney into line at the table filled with food. "He seems to find you every bit as adorable. Do you think you two kids have what it takes to really make it?" Brooke put out her arm, and in a big motion, waved Eli over to join them.

Whitney watched Eli as he was saying goodbye to his mom's friends, and looked down to pick up a paper plate. "Probably not. He's only going to be here for a few more weeks, then he's going to leave, just like—" She couldn't even finish the sentence. What in the world was she doing, opening herself up to so much heartbreak?

But then, as she was scooping up a spoonful of potato salad, an arm swept around her waist and Eli whispered, "Miss me?" His mouth was next to her ear, his breath tickling her neck and sending goosebumps down her arms.

Whitney turned to him, grinning. "Nah. I was enjoying being a respectable enough distance away, in the middle of a crowd, so I could just admire you standing there in a suit and making your mom so happy, and have it not look so obvious."

Eli glanced back at his mom, a look of conflict crossing his face, before turning to Brooke and holding out his hand. "Hi, I'm Eli. I'm guessing you're Brooke."

Brooke shook his hand. "Nice to meet the man who got Whitney to go on a date for the first time in... How long has it been? Three years?"

Whitney shot Brooke a look that she hoped conveyed a threat of monumental proportions if she brought that up again.

Eli placed a fried chicken drumstick on his plate. "I feel an odd mix of honor and fear of messing it up."

"As you should," Brooke said, pointing the Jell-O spoon at him. "You take good care of my friend."

"Will do," he said, giving Whitney a smile that made her heart feel as wobbly as the Jell-O on Brooke's plate.

Monday evening, Whitney and Eli stepped into With a Cherry on Top, the ice cream shop at the far end of Main Street, near the area they were going to designate for parking during Fall Market. The owners, Marcus and Joselyn, had their backs to the door and didn't notice when they first walked in. A couple of families were sitting at different tables, enjoying their ice cream, while Marcus and Joselyn stood by the end of the counter, Joselyn holding their little baby. Marcus was making faces at the six month old, making her squeal with laughter. Whitney watched the family, and wondered if that would ever be possible for her.

The thought caught her off guard. She'd seen them with their baby a million times, and had always loved seeing them, but never before had the thought crossed her mind that it could ever be her with the husband and the baby. It had always been something that wasn't ever going to be in the cards for her. Could it be possible?

Marcus turned around just then. "Whitney! Eli!" His cheerful voice boomed through the shop. "Sorry I didn't see you walk in. What can I get for you?"

Whitney looked through the glass at the dozen canisters of ice cream, trying to decide. She'd tasted every single one of them before, which made her choice both easier and more difficult. Eli looked at the flavors too, slipping his hand into hers as they looked. It was such a small motion, yet it still zinged excitement up her arm. "I'll have a scoop of 'By the Sea Salt Honey Darling.'"

"You definitely can't go wrong with sea salt and honey," Marcus said as he scooped the ice cream over and over into a perfect ball and put it on top of a sugar cone. Then he topped it with a maraschino cherry. "And what about you, Eli? Can I get you a sample of anything?"

Whitney wondered how it was for Eli to be back in a town where at least half the people knew his name, but only from when they knew him as a rambunctious kid, an awkward middle-schooler, or a troubled high-schooler. Hopefully they would all get to know the amazing adult he'd turned into.

"No need for a sample," Eli said. "I'll take 'C is for Cookie Monster.'"

Whitney smiled as Marcus scooped up Eli's vibrant blue ice cream, filled with Oreo and chocolate chip cookie chunks, and topped it with a cherry.

When they got back onto the street, licking their ice cream and still walking hand-in-hand, Whitney said, "Do you ever miss living here?"

Eli nodded. "Sure I do. There's a different pace of life that..." He seemed to be struggling to find a way to explain it. "I don't know. It just leaves more time for people, I guess. Living in Sacramento feels like being an only child, which of course made it feel like home. But I'd forgotten how much I loved living in a big family like Nestled Hollow."

Whitney smiled. True, he'd said that Sacramento felt like home, and that's where his life was. But it was nice to hear that he also loved Nestled Hollow. But talking more about it felt dangerous, so she changed the subject to what they'd actually come here to discuss.

"So we'll put one of the arches right there at the opening to this road, by the clock tower," Whitney said, pointing with her ice cream. "And another on the other side of the street. Then we'll put two down at the other ends and two where Center crosses through Main." The sun was just setting, the sunset throwing brilliant colors across the world, the cool, crisp air smelling faintly of pine.

"They aren't very wide, though. We need something to block off the street more, so it's clear that cars can't drive on it."

"Oh!" Whitney said. "Bo Charleston texted this morning and asked if we wanted to use any of his hay bales this year. How about we put them from the sidewalk to the arch and from the arch to the creek on all four? I could have him drop off half a dozen at the sides of the building at With a Cherry on Top, half a dozen at the city building, and then another half a dozen at Treanor's and half a dozen at Back Porch Grill by Friday evening. Maybe even some at the corners of Center and Main."

"Sounds good, Honey Darling."

"I thought so, too, Cookie Monster."

Eli said, "Mmm Cookies!" and took a big bite of his ice cream. After swallowing, he said, "I don't care if this turns my entire mouth blue—it's the best ice cream I've had in my life."

"Eli!" Mike Carter said as he neared them on the sidewalk. "I heard you were back in town. How you doing, buddy? You two staying out of trouble?"

Whitney could tell that the question really bothered Eli, but he didn't show it to Mike. He greeted the man who was only five years older than they were, but who was already managing the convenience store they used to frequent when they were in high school, and chatted with him.

His mood had changed, though, and after Mike left, Whitney said, "Okay, to be fair, we were a couple of punk kids."

"I know. And the more they see the adult me, the less they'll judge me as the punk kid." He said it, though, like it was some line that he wasn't sure he believed. "How many strands of lights are we going to string between the buildings?"

Whitney looked up. "We've done it before at Christmastime with fifty or one hundred strands, and both ways looked good. What do you think?"

"Since people will need to see the things in the vendor booths, I say the more light the better. That way, vendors won't feel the need to provide their own lighting, and the strands above will look better." He hesitated for a moment, and then added, "But it'll take hours and hours to hang fall leaves from a hundred strands of lights. How many people do you think you can rustle up to help?"

"As many as we need." Whitney shrugged. "What do you think— a couple dozen?"

Eli stopped walking and just looked at her. She wasn't sure why, so she just licked her ice cream and stared into his beautiful eyes rimmed with those amazing dark lashes.

"You're incredible. You know that, right?"

Whitney wrinkled her brow, confused.

Eli laughed. "You just go around, being amazing, and don't even realize, do you?" He leaned forward and kissed her forehead.

Whitney took the opportunity with him standing so close, holding his ice cream cone, to lean forward and take a bite of his. "You're right," she said through the mouthful. "This is pretty tasty ice cream."

He bopped her on the nose with his ice cream cone in retaliation, then, still standing so close and smelling fantastic, his eyes went from her eyes to her nose. "No," she said, reaching around him and grabbing one of the napkins he had sticking out of his back pocket. "You are not licking this off my nose." She wiped off the ice cream, not taking her eyes off his, with the exception of that moment when she let her eyes go to his lips. Then stood on her tip toes and kissed him.

They turned back to the sidewalk, and kept walking, amid all the Monday evening shoppers.

"When do vendors usually set up their booths?" Eli asked.

"Friday afternoon or evening. Some do early on Saturday morning. We could ask for volunteers to come help Friday afternoon, before it gets dark. Maybe we could even talk Cole at Back Porch Grill into letting us use the empty side of his building. There's enough room in there that we could keep working even after it got dark."

They both tossed the last bit of their ice cream cones into their mouths at the same time.

"Perfect. I think we should wait to put the leaves down on the road until early Saturday morning, though. That way they'll be fresh and not stepped on when Fall Market opens."

They stopped in front of the Gazette and Eli looked up at the building. Whitney looked up at it, too, as if seeing it through Eli's eyes. The truth was, she hardly ever actually stopped and looked up at the face of this gray stone building that looked like it had always been there and always would be. The architecture was actually rather beautiful. A stone archway was perfectly centered on the building, rising above the front doors. Stone columns rose at the sides, with crenellations on top, like a castle.

Eli walked forward and placed his hand on the shoulder of a bronze bust of Mr. Annesley that the town had placed on a pedestal in the middle of the sidewalk not long after his death. He read from the plaque at the base of the bust, "'In honor of Joseph Annesley, founder of the Nestled Hollow Gazette. Joseph did more to bring the town of Nestled Hollow together, cheering one another's accomplishments and supporting one another in grief than anyone in our town's history. His constant smile, kind words, and ever presence will be missed.' Wow. That's very... Whitney, what's wrong?"

Whitney's breaths came in heaving gasps, yet she couldn't seem to get enough air. She didn't think about Mr. Annesley. She never allowed herself to remember how he'd been like a father to her when hers passed away. That he'd always believed in her, even when no one else had. That he and his wife had been her family when she was still in college and suddenly had no family left in Nestled Hollow. That he gave her the confidence she would need to be able to run the paper by herself. That he promised to teach her everything she needed to know, and be there to support her after he retired, and answer any questions that came up. And then he suddenly wasn't there and all his promises to help meant nothing, because he was gone. She never *ever* allowed herself to think about these things. Eli had somehow gotten her to open a crack in her wall, and now everything came flooding in.

The tears ran down her face, and Eli wrapped his arms around her, strong and protective. "No," she said, pushing him away. "I can't. I can't do this." She couldn't open her heart to one more person, just to have them gone from her life much too soon. "I've— I'm sorry. I have to go."

She ran around to the back of the building, knowing she was leaving Eli standing on the sidewalk, bewildered, but unable to do anything about it. She fumbled in her purse for her keys, hopped into her car, and raced to 9th Street and her apartment.

Her apartment felt even more empty than usual. She paced back and forth from the couch in her living room, around the small table in her kitchen, and back to the couch. She needed to talk to someone. Not Eli. Not just someone from town. She needed to talk to someone about everything that had come inside the wall she'd carefully built around her heart. And she never let people from town inside that wall.

Brooke. She was from town, but she was also her best friend. She picked up her phone and sent her a text.

ARE YOU FREE FOR A LATE DINNER TONIGHT? OR LUNCH TOMORROW?

It only took a few seconds for a return text.

SORRY, SWEETIE! I'M JUST FINISHING PACKING RIGHT NOW, AND THEN I'M RACING OFF TO CATCH A 9PM FLIGHT TO NYC. YOU'LL NEVER BELIEVE IT—THAT DESIGNER FROM L.A., IZIC VEGA, ACTUALLY RECOMMENDED ME TO A FAMOUS DESIGNER, AND THEY WANT TO MEET ME IN PERSON! I'LL BE BACK ON FRIDAY. DINNER THEN?

She typed out *That's great! I'm excited for you! Dinner Friday then*, then pressed send and tossed her phone on the couch. People left. That's just the way it was— a fact of life. She knew that better than anyone. She didn't know why she ever thought it would be okay to open her wall a crack. She had to protect herself, and the one way to do that was to keep that wall around her heart strong and impenetrable.

Chapter Sixteen

*E*li rushed into Treanor's, knowing that Grace needed to leave soon to take her son to a doctor's appointment, and that Max had school on Tuesdays.

"You're not wet," she said as he approached the counter. "Did you not get the canoe righted and back to shore?"

Eli tried not to let his annoyance show. There were customers in the shop, after all. "When they said they 'capsized' their boat, they didn't actually mean that it flipped over and they couldn't get it righted. They meant that they sunk it to the bottom of the lake."

Grace gasped. "Are they going to pay for it?"

"Not beyond the two hundred dollar damage deposit they left."

"Maybe we can get some divers to pull it up." She opened a drawer in the desk and started shuffling through papers. "Your dad has used divers before. I think there's a phone number in here."

"I'll take care of it. You're going to be late."

Grace glanced up at the clock, let out an *Eek!* and rushed

off. Eli took a long, calming breath, and then walked to a couple and their tween daughter, who were looking at the long boards. The parents were going to be renting bikes, but their daughter had always wanted to try long boarding, so he helped them get outfitted with helmets, equipment, and all the knee and shoulder pads their daughter would need to stay safe.

He hadn't even gotten to the second family in the shop, let alone finished with the first, before an angry dad stormed into the shop, pushing a bike, his teenaged son following close behind him.

"We were rented faulty equipment!"

Eli told the family he'd be right back, and then went to the man. "What happened?"

"My son and I were riding the bikes, having a great father-son bonding outing when the tire suddenly went flat. Your equipment completely ruined our excursion!"

Eli wanted to tell the man that it was probably the anger that was coming off the man in waves that ruined the excursion, but instead took a look at the tire. Both tires were filled with sticker weeds. Not enough to pop the tire, but enough to tell him that they weren't riding on the streets like they'd said they were going to. "Where did you go on your excursion?"

"We were headed along the road in front of the lake, and about a half mile past it, we saw some deer up in the mountains, and headed off through the field to get a closer look."

Eli stood up. "These bikes were made for paved roads. If you'd like to go off road, we have bikes that are perfect for that." He motioned to the row of the bikes they had with tires thick enough to handle any punishment these two were going to give it. "Would you like to rent those instead?"

"We just had to walk this blasted bike two miles back here!

We're too hot and tired to rent other bikes. I tell you what you should be doing is buying us lunch for all our troubles."

The man was bellowing everything he said, like he was trying to convince every potential customer in a three mile radius not to rent from Treanor's, when he was actually trying to get the focus off the fact that he was the one at fault. Eli wasn't interested in trying to keep anyone as a customer who would treat the equipment this badly, but he did need to calm the situation. He stepped closer to the man. In a voice quiet enough that only the man could hear, he said, "We both know this wasn't faulty equipment; it was equipment abuse. But I also understand that you and your son must be exhausted and hungry. There's a burger joint just two buildings down called Keetch's. Take your son there and I can guarantee you'll come out of this being the hero in his eyes."

The man looked at Eli, fists on his hips, breathing heavy, like he was trying to decide if he was going to shout some more, throw a punch, or listen to Eli. After a few tense moments, the man gave a curt nod, and turned and left with his son.

The day continued on as it started— the shop filled with tourists who came into town early for the Fall Market, and customer after customer complaining. There wasn't even a long enough break for Eli to grab a single bite from the sandwich he had brought for lunch. He'd helped out plenty of times in the store as a teenager during the week of Fall Market, but it had never been this busy, and they never had just one person manning the whole shop by themselves.

The afternoon had been a whirlwind of problem after problem, not even giving him a chance to breathe in between. He'd just finished up with a customer who had been mad that they'd gotten lost when they took a side-by-side up to look at the fall leaves. The tourist complained that there should've been better trail markings. Eli pointed out that he'd given them a map, but the customer complained because the area they were in wasn't even on the map. Eli wanted to say that the fact it wasn't on the map should've been their first clue not to go that way, and instead used what was likely the very last bit of patience he could tap into and calmed the customers. Barely. By the time they finally left, he was ready to just lock the front doors early and go somewhere far away from everyone.

And, of course, that's when Broden Smith walked in— a local two years older than Eli who had always been a fan of trying to make Eli feel worthless. *Great.*

Eli took a deep breath before walking up to the man. "Hello, Broden. Long time no see."

"Eli! I heard you were back in town." Broden clapped him on the back. "It's good to see you, buddy. Hey, listen. It's my five year anniversary on Friday, and I really want to take my wife out on the lake. Can you hook me up with a paddle boat?"

"I can't. We're booked solid on Friday."

Broden let out a low growl. "Fine. How about a canoe then?"

"They're gone, too. It's one of the last good weekends on the lake before the end of the season, and we've got tons of extra tourists in town for Fall Market. There's not much of anything left."

Broden narrowed his eyes at Eli. "Are you just saying you won't rent to me to get even for all the times I razzed you in high school? I mean grow up, Eli! Act like a man, and not like a high school drama queen."

Heat rushed to Eli's face and his hands clenched at his sides. He stepped up close to Broden and said slowly, so

Broden couldn't miss anything, "I'm saying I won't rent to you because I have nothing to rent."

"Come on, Eli. Figure something out! Find me something."

"What are you expecting? That I'll just let a tourist who booked a paddle boat months ago know that sorry, they can't have their reservation any longer, and give it to you instead?"

"That would be awesome. Thanks."

Eli ground his teeth as he reached for a reserve of patience — anything at all— but came up empty. His heart pounded, heat flushing through his body. "I am not going to jerk one of our customers around just because you didn't think to get a reservation for your anniversary until two days before."

Broden's nostrils flared. He widened his stance and threw an arm out to the side, gesturing to the equipment in the room. "Your father would've given me the reservation, even if I'd come in the day of. He would've figured something out, *and* would've given me the local discount to boot! He wouldn't have given me some sorry excuse by a *sorry. Excuse. Of. A. Man.*" Broden punctuated each word with a jab of his finger into Eli's chest.

"Out." Eli pointed to the door. "Get out, and I better not see your face in here again."

Eli's breathing was ragged as Broden stormed out the door, slamming it behind him. His heart was pounding so hard, he couldn't focus on anything; he just stared in the general direction of the door, working to calm his breathing.

Until his father came out from behind a display of swim toys. Eli hadn't even heard him come in. His dad rolled to him, his booted foot hanging off the end of a knee scooter, his expression fuming. "Is this how you treat all of my customers? By yelling at them and throwing them out of my store?"

"I don't treat all of them like that," Eli yelled back. "Just the ones who act like entitled jerks!"

His mom walked into the store just then, all smiles, until she saw Eli's and his dad's expressions.

"I don't know how you've managed to keep your own business if this is how you deal with problems! I should've never trusted you to run things while I recovered. We should've never dragged you back."

"That seems to be the common consensus around here."

"Oh, honey," Eli's mom said. "You don't mean that. And you, Robert," she said, turning to his dad, "definitely don't mean that."

"No, I do," his dad said. "I should come back to work right this—" He stepped down from the scooter but then winced in pain, bending over.

His mom put her arm around his dad, talking to him in a calm voice, reminding him about his blood pressure, adjusting his leg back onto the scooter while Eli took a few pacing steps, trying to work out the anger out of his system. Then she turned to Eli. "You're doing a fine job, honey. Really. Please keep it up." Then she directed his dad back out the front door.

Eli closed his eyes, taking a few slow breaths, and then glanced up at the clock. Five forty-nine. All the equipment was returned, and it was close enough to six that he didn't feel the least bit guilty about closing early. He grabbed the keys from behind the counter, and had almost made it to the front door when Evia, an older woman who had even fluffier hair now than she had when he was a kid, walked in. Not his usual type of customer at all.

"Good evening, Evia," he said, trying to show something that resembled a welcoming smile. Or just a smile in general. It was probably more of a grimace. "How can I help you?"

"Hello, Eli. Good to see you again. I'm actually here about Whitney."

Despite his exhaustion, Eli stood up straighter in surprise.

"I saw the two of you holding hands on Main Street last night, just like when you were kids."

He nodded, unsure of where Evia was going with this. Although he had run though the events of last night in his head a million times since then, he still hadn't quite figured out what to think about Whitney's reaction to the sculpture of Mr. Annesley, or what she had meant when she told him "I can't do this." He was torn between trying to give her space, and wanting to just talk with her to see what was wrong. To find out why reading the tribute out loud had made her so upset. If the day hadn't been so busy, he knew that talking with her would've won out. It had been nearly twenty-four hours since he'd last seen her, and he was aching to be with her again. He wanted to make sure that she was okay. And after a day like today, being with her, knowing that she was okay, sounded like heaven.

"Now I know I'm just someone from town who don't got no business butting myself into yours, but we love Whitney. You know we all love Whitney, right?"

Eli nodded.

"And we want what's best for her. Now I'm not saying that you're not what's best for her. All I'm sayin' is that last time you left without so much as a how-ya-doin' phone call after, you might as well have reached in, pulled her heart out, threw it on the ground and stomped on it for all the harm it did that girl."

A lump formed in Eli's throat and heat prickled up his neck and on his face. If how badly he felt when he'd left before was any indication at all, he had a pretty good idea of how Whitney had felt. What was he doing, falling for her and hoping she felt the same all over again, when he had no intention of staying? What kind of person did that make him?

She reached out and held his hand in one of hers, patting his hand with her other hand. "I can see in your eyes you care about her and wouldn't want nothin' bad to happen when you left again. So I thought you should know what happened last time."

"Thanks for letting me know," he muttered, and sunk down with his back against the counter as Evia walked out the door.

Luckily, no one else walked through the door while Eli sat there, feeling every bit of everyone's frustrations, fury, and worry pressing down on him. Eventually, he got up, locked the front door, grabbed the sandwich out of the employee fridge that he had hoped to eat six hours ago, and took a big bite out of it as he was heading out the back door to his car. The books could wait until tomorrow.

His phone rang. He pulled it out of his pocket, saw that it was Ben, and answered before he even finished chewing. "Hey." He swallowed. "Man, you don't know how good it is to hear the voice of someone who doesn't want to run me out of town."

"Going that well, huh?"

Eli made a grunting, mumbled sound that probably couldn't have been interpreted as actual words as he took another bite of the sandwich.

"Well, how about I share some good news then?"

"I'm listening," Eli said through a mouthful, knowing that Ben wouldn't judge him for letting his stomach take precedence on a day like today.

"Smithfield Corporate called."

Eli swallowed and stopped walking, unable to do anything

other than listen. "Smithfield? Please tell me you're not joking right now."

"Scout's honor, I'm telling the absolute truth. How many months have we been schmoozing them, and then after we finally give up, they call us."

"And? You're killing me here, Ben."

"And they want to meet to talk about sending us all twenty-five hundred employees from their corporate office, over a total of six weeks."

"Wow. Wow! This is incredible."

"If things go well, they may want to talk about us training the people at their district offices, too."

Eli couldn't believe this. He and Ben had been working so hard to grow their business. They'd made great progress, but they both knew they needed a big break— like training a Fortune 500 company. A success like that could mean they wouldn't have to go to businesses and convince them to use TeamUp; the businesses would come to them. "Why do I feel like there's a 'but' waiting in the wings?"

"Because they won't meet with only me. They want us as a team, in their offices, this Friday."

Eli ran his hand through his hair and leaned against his car. "I can't. My dad won't be cleared by the doctor to head back to work for at least two weeks— maybe quite a few more, and I'm kind of co-in charge of a thing on Saturday. Can they move it at all? Even next week would be better."

"No can do. Their Chief Operations officer wants to get things rolling before he leaves for Africa for a month late Friday night. Is there any way to make it work? It could be a quick trip. You fly home Thursday night, we go to the meeting Friday morning, and you can hop back on a plane by Friday afternoon. And besides, it sounds like you could really use a break from Nestled Hollow."

Eli paused. There had to be a way he could make this work. "My dad's so full of pent up energy and worry about how I'm running his company into the ground, by two days from now, he'd probably jump at the chance to take over. And even if my mom wouldn't let him, I'm sure he's at the point where he doesn't need her to be there constantly. She ran the shop with him; she could probably run the place on her own even if he couldn't. The assistant manager here is quite capable, too."

"Great! One thing down. I'm getting on the website to buy you plane tickets as we speak. Now what about this thing you're in charge of?"

"It's the decorations for an event here called Fall Market. It's kind of a big deal."

"And can your 'co-in charge' person handle it without you?"

Eli thought about all the planning they'd done, and how much he wanted to put all of it together with Whitney. And how disappointed she would be if he said he had to leave. How disappointed *he* would be if he had to leave. But if he could get an early enough flight back on Friday, she wouldn't have to do too much of it on her own. And she already said she could get practically the whole town to help.

"She could definitely handle it on her own." He was pretty sure she could marshal enough people at the snap of her fingers to accomplish pretty much anything.

"I feel a 'but' waiting in the wings." Eli heard a big clap sound come from the other end of the phone. "It's her! It's the girl you told me about, isn't it. What was her name?"

"Whitney."

"Oh, wow. I didn't think you'd actually take me up on the

'Come home broken hearted' thing. This is big. Like *Smithfield* big."

"Don't get so excited. I don't think it's going to work out." He pushed himself upright and turned and unlocked his car door, then opened it and tossed his half-eaten, wrapped sandwich on the passenger's seat.

"Ahh. I see. You've hit the two week mark with her. She's just like every other girl."

"She's not even in the same ballpark."

"I can't wait to hear all about her. If you can get things worked out for the fall decoration thing and with your parents, there's an empty seat on a Delta flight out of Denver Thursday at seven twenty. That work?"

"Thursday at seven twenty on Delta. Gotcha." Eli got into his car, shut the door, and turned the ignition. "I'll go talk with my parents right now, and then I'll talk with Whitney."

"I picked a nice center seat for you. I'm pretty sure it's right between a crying baby and a man who hasn't showered in three weeks. Should be a grand time."

Eli laughed, and after a day like today, it felt good. But it only lasted for a moment before his thoughts went back to Whitney. "And Ben? She is *not* like every other girl. She's far too amazing for the likes of me."

Chapter Seventeen

uring the hours Whitney was at work by herself this morning, she got the sum total of zero things done. Now that Kara and Scott were there, each with articles for her to edit and questions for her to answer, and random people stopped in with stories of things that happened in town to report, her mind actually got moments to focus on things other than Eli and the look that was on his face when she'd run away from him last night.

But now, Scott and Kara were busy writing articles, and Whitney was staring at the layout on her computer screen once again, unable to make any decisions on what to put where, because her mind kept wandering.

Her phone rang, and she slid to answer the call. "Hi, Mom. Is everything okay?"

"Just because I don't usually call you on a Tuesday afternoon doesn't mean anything's wrong."

"Oh, then hi. How are you doing?"

"But it doesn't mean that I didn't call because I have news."

"Oh, great! I could use some good news today."

"Then you'll be happy to hear that our local newspaper, the Willow Grove Weekly, is looking for someone to run the paper. I know the owners and after I chatted with them— lovely couple— we've decided that you're perfect for the job."

"Mom."

"Now honey, listen. Every time you come visit, you say how much you love Willow Grove, and the town really needs someone like you to really bring the community together, and I know if you were running the paper, that's exactly what would happen."

"*Mom.*"

"You wouldn't have to give up ownership of the Nestled Hollow Gazette. The Weekly wouldn't need you here for a full two months, which is plenty of time for you to train someone to run the Gazette for you. Then you could just check on them every day via email, and fly back to Nestled Hollow once a month or so and see how it's doing in person. Would you like me to set up an interview with the owners for you?"

"I love you, Mom."

"Is that a yes?"

"It's a 'thanks for looking out for me.' Come on, Mom, you know it's a *no*. Nestled Hollow has my heart; it always has." She loved her mom and Jackie and Jackie's husband and her niece and nephew. She wished they never moved away. Nestled Hollow felt exactly like family, but she always wished she had actual blood family here, too.

Her mom sighed. "Well, it didn't hurt to ask. Let me know if you change your mind."

"I will," she said, and after they told each other goodbye, she hung up the phone.

She reached out and picked up the swan that Eli had made her from the paper napkin at Keetch's and turned it over and over. Last night had been rough. If Eli and she hadn't just gone out for ice cream, it definitely would've been a curl-up-on-the-couch-with-Ben-and-Jerry's night. Not that she had any ice cream in her freezer. Or food in her house in general, other than some breakfast bars, microwave popcorn, and half a quart of milk that was probably expired. She definitely needed to keep more food in her house. Maybe even spend more than thirty minutes of awake time there each day.

She had hoped that after a good night's sleep, her emotions would've calmed down. That she wouldn't be so freaked out about everything. But the truth was, she was pretty darn experienced at having people that she loved leave her. She knew exactly how it went, and definitely knew better than to get involved with Eli in the first place.

But at the same time, it was Eli. Could she really have expected herself not to see him at all? After twelve years of wanting to see him? She needed to find out where he was at and what his plans were. Because if his plans were to just stay here for the next two to four weeks then leave this town in the dust, she needed to wean her heart off him now, so it wouldn't be so painful when he left. She knew exactly how much damage he could do to her heart, and she needed to do everything she could to protect herself now. What had she been thinking, opening her heart again when all signs pointed to things ending badly?

She looked at the clock in the corner of her computer screen. Five fifty-five. Treanor's would be closing in just five minutes— now might be the perfect time to go. She could slip in right at closing, and then they could chat afterward.

"Scott and Kara?" Both staff writers looked up as she grabbed her blazer and slipped her arms into the sleeves. "I've got to run an errand. If I don't make it back before it's time for you to leave, just email me your articles."

They both nodded, and she walked out the door and headed down Main Street toward Treanor's. When she got to the shop, though, the doors were already locked, and the lights were off. She headed down the alley between Treanor's and the bakery, to see if Eli's car was in the parking lot still. As she neared the end of the alley, though, she heard his voice, then a pause, then his voice again. He must be on the phone. She almost stepped out into the parking lot, but paused, deciding that he'd probably feel like he had to end his phone call if he saw her. She wasn't in a hurry— she'd give him just a moment.

"My dad's so full of pent up energy and worry about how I'm running his company into the ground, by two days from now, he'd probably jump at the chance to take over. And even if my mom wouldn't let him, I'm sure he's at the point where he doesn't need her to be there constantly. She ran the shop with him; she could probably run the place on her own even if he couldn't. The assistant manager here is quite capable, too."

Whitney hadn't meant to eavesdrop, but Eli was talking plenty loud enough for her to hear. Was he really talking about leaving? Just *two days* from now? Whatever happened to two to four weeks from now? She was too shocked by his words to go out where he could see her, or to walk away. She just stood there, frozen.

"It's the decorations for this event here called Fall Market. It's kind of a big deal."

Yeah, it kind of was a big deal. To the entire town. She had thought it was a big deal to her and Eli as well.

"She could definitely handle it on her own."

A lump in her stomach started forming as she pictured

doing the rest of the preparations without him. About doing the rest of everything in her life without him.

"Whitney," he said, and paused before saying words that would burn themselves into her brain forever. "Don't get so excited. I don't think it's going to work out."

The punch to her gut felt so literal she sunk against the side of the building.

She heard him open his car door before adding the next punch. "She's not even in the same ballpark. Thursday at seven twenty on Delta. Gotcha." She heard his car door shut, the engine start, then sounds of Eli driving away.

She couldn't believe he was going to leave in just two days. Why would he change his plans so drastically without even mentioning it to her first? Had their last two weeks together meant so much less to him than it had to her?

It took several long minutes before she could even process it all enough to push herself upright. Eventually, she made it back to the paper and sank down into her office chair, staring off at nothing.

"Whitney? Are you okay?"

Whitney shook herself more alert and focused on Kara. "I'm fine," she lied, and then moved her mouse to bring her screen back to life. She moved it around a bit, making it look like she was working, but then gave up and just stared at the napkin swan. How many times was she going to have to relearn this same lesson? Letting people in was dangerous. Loving people was dangerous. She'd had plenty of alarms going off in her head since the moment she'd seen Eli in that Main Street Business Alliance meeting, and had chosen to ignore them over and over. Even though she knew in her core that she shouldn't have. She had walls in place for this very purpose.

Thirty minutes later, a text came in. She glanced down at her phone. It was Eli.

WANT TO GO FOR AN EVENING STROLL AROUND THE LAKE? SAY, 8:00?

He didn't mention why, but she already knew— he wanted to meet so he could tell her that he was leaving her once again, with barely any more notice than he had given her the last time.

Chapter Eighteen

On his way to his parents' house, Eli had called Grace and Max to make sure they were able to work until closing on Thursday, since he would need to be gone by just before five. When he got to his parents' house, he was surprised at how well they reacted to him asking if they could run the store on Friday. They weren't sure if his dad would be able to be in the store more than an hour, but his mom sounded more than confident enough to run it without him for just a day.

Now he just needed to get Whitney on board. That wasn't going to be so easy— he knew that she'd be able to get the help she needed, since everyone seemed to be willing to drop what they were doing to help her, but he also knew that the event meant a lot to her. Truth be told, he was sad he was going to have to miss out on the preparations on Friday.

As he drove to the lake, he ran through dialogue in his head about how to best bring the subject up to Whitney, trying out different things, hoping he could figure out the best way. As it usually was after dark, the parking lot at the lake was empty, so he pulled into one of the closest spots to the trail, right under a street lamp. He got out, and even though he was wearing his jacket, he shivered in the cold autumn air and zipped up his jacket.

He was pulling a couple of flashlights out of his trunk when Whitney pulled into the lot and parked. The moment she got out of the car, he knew everything wasn't okay. The happy expression that usually lived on her face even when she wasn't smiling was gone. Something was wrong.

He took two strides to close the distance between them. He'd started to raise his arms to wrap them around her, but she put her hands into her pockets and turned to the side, so he dropped his arms and asked, "Is everything okay? Are you still upset about last night?" He couldn't believe that through the craziness of the day, he hadn't texted her or checked in on her to make sure she was okay. She had been so upset last night, and didn't seem to want him to follow her then, but today he should've gone to her.

"I'm fine. It's just been a rough day. What about you?" She reached out a hand toward him, like she was going to put her hand on his arm, but pulled back before she did. "Are you okay? What's wrong?"

"Same," he said. "It's just been a rough day."

She nodded, and he handed her a flashlight. "I hear walks around the lake can undo rough days, though."

"Please let it be so," Whitney softly said as she turned and led them down the trail to the lake.

As they neared the lake, Eli went through all the different ways he was going to start off the conversation, trying to settle on one. Before he opened his mouth to start off the conversation, Whitney turned to him and said, "Tell me what

135

happened between our graduation ceremony and the all-nighter."

Eli was caught completely off guard by the request. His mind had gone a million places today, and this definitely hadn't been one of them.

"Please," she said. "It's important. I really want to understand."

Whitney had always been someone who called him out on things. She didn't just keep her mouth shut if she didn't agree with something, or if he was making a stupid choice. As much as he'd been dreading the moment when she asked, he was actually surprised she hadn't demanded he tell her sooner.

He gave a single nod, and turned onto the sandy beach that encircled the lake, shining the flashlight on the ground in front of them as they walked. "I haven't actually told anyone the story." He cleared his throat, trying to decide how to start. "I'm sure you remember how my dad responded to the separation between him and my mom with drinking and depression, and how he took it out on me. I was convinced there wasn't a single small part of him that loved me. If it weren't for my mom and for you, especially, I'm not sure I would've made it through my junior and senior year. I was counting down the days until we'd leave."

He turned to Whitney, meeting her eyes in the moonlight. "I had planned to stay here for the summer after high school and go to Denver University with you, just like we'd planned. I swear to you that I had."

She searched his eyes, like she was trying to see if she found truth there, her body slightly shivering in the cold air. She must've decided that she had, because then she turned and kept walking.

He took a deep breath and walked alongside her, his feet

sinking into the sand with each step. "I had given up trying to make my dad proud of me long before, since it only seemed to make him even more critical. Why try when he was impossible to please? And my dad can only love someone he's proud of, so that's why I spent most of the time staying at my mom's apartment. And all the time I could with you."

He smiled at the memory. If he only thought of Whitney, he had the best high school experience anyone could ask for. If he thought of everything else, it was the worst. "Until things got bad even with her leading up to graduation, you two made me feel like maybe I was actually someone worth loving." The admission came out as a whisper. He hadn't even meant to admit that at all to anyone ever. That worry was still too much a part of who he was now, and it was too raw to say. He wished he could take it back. He almost turned around right then and walked back to his car, but Whitney reached out and put her hand on his arm.

He couldn't have her looking at him while he talked, so he turned and started walking alongside the lake again. "Then, after the graduation ceremony, when most graduates were off having celebratory meals with their families, my mom and I got into the biggest argument we'd ever had. I guess she was sick of me slacking off, and we both said some pretty harsh things. In my mind, she was no longer the safe parent who loved me no matter what— she had revealed that she felt the same way about me that my dad had, she had just been nicer about it. So I went into my room, slammed my door, and packed up all my stuff.

"While I was loading everything I owned into my car, I suddenly knew that Denver wasn't far enough away. Being close enough to see them every weekend wouldn't do it. I needed to go somewhere where I could just get lost among people who wouldn't care whether I was my parents' ideal son or not." They'd made it to the west end of the small lake, where it was curving around to the side. He was glad that they were walking—talking about all this reminded him how strongly that need to run was.

He had tried talking her into going with him. He'd told her they could still keep their same plans—staying in dorms at college—but going to a different college. One in California. But she'd tried just as fiercely to talk him into still going to the University of Denver. After a debate that was much too short for as much as it would change their lives, he'd said he was going to California no matter what, and really wanted her to join him. She'd said no.

"I was fresh off the fight with my mom, feeling raw and hurt that she didn't love me either, and obviously didn't tell you that I needed to leave in the best way ever, because you were so mad. Do you remember how angry you were?"

"Of course I do," she whispered, and he realized that she'd probably replayed it in her own head just as often as he had.

"Do you remember what you told me?" She didn't respond, so he said, "You said, 'Fine then, go. I don't care if you leave.'" His throat tightened, and he paused a long moment, making sure that his voice wouldn't crack when he spoke again. "Those were the exact same words my mom had said just a couple of hours earlier. Which made me feel like you felt the same way about me— that I wasn't worth loving."

One of the chaperones, someone who had given him almost as much grief as his dad did, had noticed the exchange and asked him to leave before either of them had said another word. So he left. No one in this town had wanted him there anyway.

Whitney opened her mouth to say something, but he held

up a hand. "I know it wasn't your fault that I left. I knew that I had hurt you, and that you didn't actually feel that way about me. Well, I didn't know it at the time. At the time, I one hundred percent believed you didn't want me there. I stayed that night in Denver, slept in my car, and woke up the next morning and kept driving and eventually found myself in central California. It wasn't until I was there that everything finally caught up to me. That's when I realized that you actually did love me, and that I had just run away from the best thing in my life."

They were silent as they walked, staring out at how the moon and stars bounced off the surface of the lake, making wavy, moving versions of themselves.

They had only taken half a dozen steps when Whitney stopped, hands on her hips, and said, "So why didn't you ever call? You were my *best friend*, Eli. My best friend, *and* my boyfriend, and you just left without a backward glance. If you had figured out that I was the best thing in your life, why didn't you call?"

Eli hung his head. He had gone back over things in his mind a million times since then, and he'd always come up with the same conclusion. "Because I was a stupid prick of a kid, who turned into a stupid prick of an adult."

"Not a good enough answer."

He knew it wasn't. And he knew she'd call him out on it. "The first time I tried calling was when I found out that my parents had turned my cell service off, hoping that would make me come back home. But I just couldn't. I had too many things to figure out about myself, and too many things to prove. I found a job there working at a burger joint and slept in my car every night until I saved up enough to get a real place."

He blew out a big breath. This was hard stuff to admit—

no wonder he hadn't told a soul. Not even Ben knew the whole story. "Every time my fingers itched to pick up the phone just so I could hear your voice again, the stupid prideful part of me thought about how embarrassing my living conditions were, and how I should prove that I could make it on my own first. I told myself I could call when I was standing on my own two feet. And then the longer time went on, the more successful I thought I had to be to justify how long it had been since I called. Until before long, it had been so long that it felt impossible to ever be successful enough." He scoffed. "Saying that out loud makes it sound even stupider." It was painful looking back at this part of his life. He'd just kept making one bad choice after another.

He glanced over at Whitney, and saw silent tears running down her face. "Oh, Whitney," he said, cupping her face in his hands, wiping her tears away with his thumbs. "I am so sorry I hurt you." He had imagined a million times how badly he had hurt her by leaving when they were teens. Seeing it in person was so much worse. How could he have done this to her?

"And now you're just leaving again." She pushed his hands off her face, and started walking again. They were a good three-fourths of the way around the lake now.

"You know already?"

"Thursday night, seven twenty, on Delta. I came to talk to you in the parking lot and heard part of your conversation. At least you're giving me two days' notice before you leave this time, instead of the thirty minutes you gave me last time."

He realized that whatever part of the conversation she had heard hadn't included the part where he was only going to be gone until late Friday night. He opened his mouth to correct her, but then shut it again. If he came back after his meeting on Friday and stayed as long as his parents wanted him to stay, he would still be leaving permanently in just a few weeks. If he came back for those few weeks, he would want to be around Whitney the whole time. He'd wanted to be around her every moment for the past fourteen years, after all— the only thing that had kept him away was 1100 miles across four states and a whole lot of fear that he hadn't faced until now. His being here was hurting her. And the longer he waited to leave, the more damage he was going to cause. So as far as Whitney was concerned, maybe Thursday was the best time for him to leave permanently.

Instead of correcting her, he said, "I'm sorry, Whitney. I'm sorry for all the pain I caused back then, and I'm sorry for the pain I've caused by being back. I wish I could erase it all."

Whitney looked him in the eyes for a few long moments, and then she shook her head and walked a few steps away. "But see, Eli? You can't erase it all! You can't just wish things and make them true. You can't just say sorry and erase pain. You have to make the choices it takes to get the outcome you want."

"I *have* to go. There's a big company who wants to be TeamUp's client, and they'll only meet with us if Ben and I show up together to their meeting on Friday. I don't have a choice." She threw her arms up in frustration. "*You* decide what you're going to do, Eli! No one made you leave on graduation night. No one is making you leave now. You are making that choice, and wishing that it won't cause any pain is pointless."

The real reason he hadn't called in all these years was that deep down, he was afraid that his actions as a bull-headed teenager had been too awful, too selfish, too hurtful, and that Whitney would never forgive him for it. He'd never realized how much hope he'd clung to that Whitney would forget the past and welcome him back with open arms until this moment when she was actually showing how upset his actions had made her.

Eli was good at making people laugh, at making them feel good about themselves, and all the things he could manage on the surface. The reason he didn't date anyone longer than two weeks was that then they would get to know the real Eli beneath the surface. And if they got to know the real him— the very imperfect, flawed, damaged him— that they'd find out he wasn't good enough. He'd made too many bad choices to ever be good enough. He thought about what Evia had said to him in Treanor's. She was right. He wasn't good enough for her. Evia knew it, he knew it, and practically the entire town knew it.

"Some people don't get a choice about leaving loved ones behind. You've always had that choice. I'm sorry, Eli. I can't be with someone who's going to choose to leave."

And he couldn't stay when staying would cause her more pain. So he just stood there and watched as the woman he'd loved since they'd first become friends fourteen years ago walked up the trail to her car and drove away.

Chapter Nineteen

---

*W*hitney sat in the basement of the library, waiting for the Main Street Business Alliance meeting to start. It had been two days since the lake, and she still felt conflicted about the way things had gone with Eli. She'd had no problem calling him out for his crap over the years, but this felt different. She'd never done it before knowing that it would hurt him.

But breaking up with him had been the healthy thing. She knew that continuing to date Eli was only going to make his living four states away even more difficult, for both of them. She was taking care of herself; she was taking care of her heart.

If it was the healthy thing to do, though, why did it feel so awful? She had been living with a piece of her heart missing for so many years that she no longer even noticed that it was missing. Then Eli came along and filled that space so perfectly that she finally understood how her heart was supposed to feel. And now that he was gone, taking that part of her heart with him, the hole felt gaping and unbearable and wrong and excruciatingly painful. How had she ever been able to live with this feeling before?

"Is Eli coming?"

Whitney glanced up to see Macie, the woman who ran Paws and Relax. She shook her head.

"How about Brooke?"

Whitney shook her head again and tried to smile. "The seat's all yours." She was glad it was at least someone single who chose to sit next to her. She didn't think she could've handled it if Macie's sister Joselyn had sat next to her, in all her new family bliss.

As she waited for the meeting to start, Whitney looked down at her hands in her lap. Eli had only been to two Main Street Business Alliance meetings, and she hadn't even known he was there for the first one, but even so, it felt wrong to not have him there. She hadn't seen him at all over the past two days, but she'd seen evidences of him being around. The boxes of leaves that they'd gathered from the mountains and stored in his back rooms were now set out and ready for her crew to get to work in the big empty room at Back Porch Grill. He'd even gotten the keys from the town hall and brought all the lights from the storage unit and put them with the leaves. He'd moved the logs, too, in groups alongside the river, so that once they closed off the roads, they could move them to be seats around the fire pits. And he'd done every bit of it without her seeing the slightest flash of him.

"Are you okay?"

Whitney's head jerked up Macie's direction. "Oh. Yeah, I'm fine." She folded and unfolded her hands, trying to figure out what a normal person with a normal heart did with their hands, and looked up at the front, like she was paying attention, instead of letting her mind drift. She tried to think of small talk conversations she could bring up with Macie, but came up blank. Thankfully, Macie spared her from the task.

"Have you met Zeus?" Macie asked.

Whitney shook her head.

"You have to stop by Paws and Relax and see him. Not only is he the cutest thing ever, he's downright magical at helping to heal—"

Macie stopped, like she was unsure how to delicately finish the sentence, so Whitney finished for her. "At helping to heal broken hearts?"

Macie nodded. "Come anytime. You can even take her home for a night if you'd like."

Whitney smiled and said, "Thank you. Truly."

She tried to pay attention as Linda Keetch brought up different business owners and they reported on the advertising that was done, the booths that were going to be going up outside of the businesses on Main Street, and the music— a local band who was going to set up where Center Street crossed the middle of Main.

"Whitney and— it looks like we need to excuse Eli today. Whitney, do you want to let us know how the decorations are coming along?"

The last time her and Eli had been at this meeting, they'd played off each other so well when they'd stood up to give their report. Pangs of missing him stabbed even more deeply as she got up in front of everyone alone.

She took a deep breath. She'd always done everything alone. She was an expert at this. After telling all about what they had planned for the decorations, she said, "I've been texting everyone in town, letting anyone who would like to help know to come tomorrow night to work with the leaves in the side room of Back Porch Grill." She gave a nod to Cole, the owner, and said, "Thanks again, for letting us use the space. Or they can come Saturday morning at seven to help set up Main Street. Sam in facilities has agreed to be ready to help us hang the lights Saturday morning as well. All of you are welcome to set up your booths outside your stores anytime. We'll work right around you."

"Where's Eli?" Ed Keetch asked.

Linda Keetch put her hand on his leg and shushed him, but the question was already out there, and everyone was watching her for an answer.

"He had a work emergency and had to head back to Sacramento, so he'll have to miss the Fall Market."

A few sympathetic *aww*'s sounded throughout the group. The moment the meeting was over, Whitney bolted out of the building before anyone could get a chance to come up and ask her questions about him.

As she was walking back to the paper, thoughts popped into her mind of the last time she'd walked down this path, just three days ago, eating ice cream, talking about everything she was looking at right now. The statue of Mr. Annesley now made her think of Eli. So did Keetch's next door. This whole street was now covered in memories of Eli. She hurried back to her office more quickly.

Scott and Kara seemed to sense that she wasn't in a chatty mood, so they left her alone as she took off her blazer, slung it over her chair, and sat down to work.

But her mind was so far away that she couldn't seem to get it thinking anywhere near the same zone as the layouts displayed on her screen, or the half-finished article she'd stopped writing three days ago that was open in her word processor, or the expenses that needed to be added into her accounting software, or the open order page for her paper vendor. She picked up the napkin swan sitting on her desk, and ran her finger along its side and thought about when they took the canoe out on the lake after dark, looking into each other's eyes, realizing she loved him, and the lights Eli had installed around the rim of the boat bouncing off the water as the waves slowly moved around them.

She set the swan down and forced herself to think of the million things she needed to do before tomorrow. She pulled out the list of people who said they'd love to come help Friday night and counted. Twenty-one people. That was perfect. Saturday morning's setup, though— that was a little more iffy. She only had five people who had given her definite yeses. Hopefully every single one of her dozen maybes would show up. And hopefully every box of leaves would cover as much of the street as they guessed it would.

Which of course, made her think of her and Eli up on the mountain, filling the boxes. Their almost kiss when they'd first come up with the idea, and their actual kiss when they were collecting them, amidst the leaves falling down from the tree. She stood up, nearly knocking her chair over. What was up with her? She was a thirty-year-old woman, not a high school kid. With all the experience she had not dating, she should be able to not date Eli right now and be just fine. A distraction was all she needed, and with how much she'd been moping over the last few days, her to-do list was filled with plenty of those.

"Scott," she said as she walked to a stack of a dozen boxes of past issues that she had been meaning to take into the storage room. "Are you busy?"

He jumped up and said, "Nope— not busy at all," so quickly that he either was hating the article he was writing, or was a little too eager to do anything he could to get her out of her morose mood. "Want some help moving these?"

They had just picked up their third load of boxes when the door opened.

"Honey," Sherry said, out of breath and standing in the doorway. "Have I got a story for you!"

A gust of wind burst in the room just then, rustling papers all around the room, and picking up the napkin swan and blowing it off Whitney's desk. Whitney yelped, dropped her box, and lurched for it, but the wind had blown it right under Scott as he was stepping down, the box he was carrying making him oblivious to the fact that his foot came down on the swan napkin, squishing it flat.

As soon as Scott saw whatever look was on her face, though, he moved the box to the side so he could see the ground, then frowned down at the swan before recognition filled his face. "Oh no. I'm so sorry. I know that was important to you."

Whitney picked up the squashed swan. "Don't worry about it. It wasn't anyone's fault. It's just a paper napkin." If it was just a paper napkin, why was she clutching it in her hand so tightly, instead of throwing it away? She turned to Kara. "Do you mind talking with Sherry and taking notes on her story?" Then she turned to Sherry. "I'm sorry, I have to—" She tried to think of a reason that she'd have to hurry and leave, but came up blank.

Sherry walked up to Whitney, gave her hand a squeeze, and said, "You go, honey. Kara and I have got this."

Whitney grabbed her blazer and got one arm through the sleeve before opening the door and pushing the other arm in on the way out. She only made it two steps into the alley that led to her car in the lot behind the building before she changed her mind on going any further and slumped down on the pavement, her back against the stone of the building, and cried.

For the first time, she truly understood why her mom had moved away all those years ago. It was painful living in a town where everywhere you looked reminded you of lost love. She pulled her cell phone from her pocket, and typed in a text to her mother.

GO AHEAD AND SET UP THE INTERVIEW WITH THE WILLOW GROVE WEEKLY.

She glanced at the text, only pausing for a short moment, before she touched send.

Chapter Twenty

*E*li stood in the offices of Rowan Davenport, while the Smithfield Chief Operations Officer watched the training videos that he and Ben had hired a professional videographer to create. The man was all crisp lines and power pose, in charge and forceful, standing in his expensive suit alongside Eli, focusing intently on their presentation. The videos were one of the best promotional materials he and Ben had made, because it showcased so well to potential clients what they did.

When the video finished, the executive directed Ben and Eli to the area of his office with a love seat and a couple of plush chairs. The man sat in the middle of the love seat and motioned to the chairs. "*If* we signed with you, tell me what your plan of action would be with training my company."

Ben nodded to Eli, acknowledging that this was his strong suit.

"Well, Mr. Davenport, there's two ways we could go about this," Eli said. "We could plan the standard team building routine— kick it all off by meeting with all twenty-five hundred employees in five big groups over the course of a week, then meet one department or team at a time over the next six weeks. Your company's efficiency will skyrocket, and you'd be very pleased with the results."

Rowan Davenport nodded.

"Or," Eli said, excitement creeping into his voice, "we go with the plan that will have the greatest lasting impact, day in and day out, over the long haul." These were the plans he liked best— the ones tailored to each company, and not the plan the big boss usually thought of originally. "You send us your team or department with the biggest issues. The ones that argue amongst themselves the most and can't seem to work together on anything or accomplish the tasks assigned to them. You make whatever sacrifices you have to in order to be able to send all of them to us for three full days. Give us your very worst, and we'll return them being your best."

"When they come back," Ben said, "you'll see the difference. They'll feel the difference."

Mr. Davenport steepled his fingers in front of his lips. Eli continued, "Word will spread throughout the company about what the training did for that team, and it'll make everyone else excited about their own turn at TeamUp. We'll schedule the rest of the company at this office about a week and a half later to give time for word to travel and excitement to build. Then we'll do the day-long training with about four or five hundred at a time— whatever works best for the way your company naturally divides. They'll get a jump start on making improvements, and we'll work with everyone to build unity and workplace pride among the company as a whole.

"Then, we'll start taking the rest of the company, a team or department or two at a time, for one to three days each, depending on how well each team is currently working with each other, and depending on whether you're wanting them to be more unified in general, or if you're wanting them to also work on being able to work together on creative or intellectual projects."

The presentation was going perfectly. Eli was adjusting on the fly to the minuscule signs the executive probably didn't even realize he was displaying. It felt so good to be doing something he was truly good at. He'd been away too long.

"Then we can get together with you about a week after all the trainings are finished and evaluate how effective it was, and if you'd like it to be a yearly training, and whether or not you'd like to extend the training to the district offices."

Eli stopped then, waiting for a response from Mr. Davenport, but the executive just tapped his lips with his fingers, studying them. This was the part where Eli had learned not to be nervous; he knew to just sit patiently and show confidence. A few tiny nerves wound their way in, though, when he thought about how powerful this corporation was, and how many employees they had outside of this one office. He pushed those thoughts away as best as he could. This was no different from meeting with a company with ten employees.

After a long moment, where he guessed the C.O.O. was trying to see if they'd crack under his intense scrutiny, Mr. Davenport sat up straight and said, "I'm meeting with the executive team at eleven and with all managers at one. I'll present this to them then. My assistant will send to you a plan of action and a recommended schedule before I leave for Africa tonight. Then you can write up a contract, get it to my people, and I'll ensure it gets signed and back to you within three days."

Eli and Ben both stood along with Rowan Davenport and shook hands with him.

"Sounds good," Ben said. "We'll get that contract sent as soon as we hear from your assistant."

Mr. Davenport walked them to his door, and then they left, walking down the hall in silence, presentation materials in their arms. They stayed silent as they waited for the elevator doors to open. They stayed silent as they waited for the doors to close and for the elevator to descend below the executive floor.

Then they both shouted in excitement, pumping their fists in the air.

"We just got Smithfied!" Ben said. "*Smithfield!*"

"I can't believe we did it. This is huge. We pull this off and we've suddenly got a power to convince other large companies that we've only dreamed of having."

"We pull it off well," Ben added, "and we might even end up with an endorsement from Smithfield. Can you just imagine how that would look on our website?"

Eli started thinking through the implications of landing a company like Smithfield, and what that would mean for TeamUp, which naturally led to thoughts of Whitney. He was so proud of himself— between the nerves and excitement waiting in Davenport's office to giving the presentation, he'd gone a good fifty minutes without thinking of her. About the way her green eyes sparkled whenever she was thinking something mischievous, or how her hair curled forward when she tucked it behind her left ear, the way it felt when his phone lit up with a text from her, or the way her lips looked so soft and inviting and perfect. How had he not kissed her more often while he was there? Especially when kissing her sent such jolts of electricity throughout his body.

"Dude," Ben exclaimed as they walked out the Smithfield Corporate office building. "How are you not more excited?"

Eli didn't want to bring Ben down with his melancholy, especially at a time like this, so he tried to push all his heartbreak over Whitney into a corner, and tap only into his feelings about the company. He grinned. "Looks like we're going to have to grow the business a little sooner than we had planned."

"What time does your plane leave again?"

"I'm not heading back. Well, eventually, I'll have to fly back to get my car and drive it home."

"You're staying? That's fantastic!" Then Ben looked at Eli and said, "Oh. It's not fantastic." He studied Eli for a moment. "The only thing that could've caused your face to do that is Whitney. I'm so sorry, man. What happened?"

"I don't want to talk about it. What's on the docket for TeamUp? There's a group coming this afternoon, right?"

Ben nodded. "The teens from that leadership conference have their afternoon and evening with us. Come help me set up. Then we'll grab some lunch, and spend the afternoon teaching them how to stand up for themselves and others. I know the teen groups are some of your favorites."

Eli smiled. "Don't bring up Whitney, and it's a deal."

They'd already ran the Chicken in a Frying Pan relay race, where they had the teens take turns using a couple of sticks to pick up a rubber chicken and run it across the field to a frying pan. And they had them do an activity called Round Tables, where they split into groups of five. Each group went to a different table filled with seemingly random objects. Only one person in each group had the instructions, and that person couldn't touch anything—

they could only instruct the others to complete the objective before the time limit, and before switching to a new table with a new leader. And they'd fed them lots of snacks and liquids.

Now the sun was getting low in the sky, and the teens were doing the last activity at TeamUp— a game called Tallest Tower, where they were split into two groups, and each group had to build a tower as tall as they could out of blocks of different sizes and shapes that looked like blocks a toddler might play with, but were much bigger, and made of balsa wood. One team's was well over six feet high, and the other's was nearing eight.

Ben had stayed true to his word and hadn't brought up Whitney, but that didn't stop her from constantly being in Eli's mind. As the two teams worked on their towers, Eli looked around at the four acres of TeamUp fields. One side was all grass, and the other was dirt. Fences surrounded the property, but so many trees and shrubs were planted around the outside edges for shade that the fences were nearly invisible. A large wooden platform stood in the exact center of the fields where he and Ben could give instruction or use them for some activities. Large storage sheds and their offices sat near the parking lot, and a big covered pavilion stretched out next to it, where they laid out snacks for their trainees. They had worked hard on what they'd built here. Eli loved it, and was proud of what they'd accomplished.

But somehow, everything felt different now. It was like he'd been living without being able to see the color green for so long that he'd gotten used to it. It had been normal. Then he went back to Nestled Hollow and gotten to know Whitney all over again, and he could suddenly see green in all its vibrancy and shades and tones, and could see what the color green brought to everything all around him. It was like seeing a color that breathed life into his soul.

And now that he was back in Sacramento without Whitney, it was like the green was gone. It hadn't been here when he'd left, but now that he knew what it was like to have it, everything felt different. Now that he knew what he was missing, he longed for it, and wasn't sure how he was ever going to live without it again.

Ben seemed to get that if Eli went home after the teens left, that he'd have too much time to spend doing nothing more than thinking of Whitney and wishing things were different, so he insisted that they go grab some dinner, then join up with a larger group of their friends to rock climb at an indoor facility, before teaming up to play laser tag.

Eli had only agreed to the plan because he knew that getting Ben to accept no for an answer was going to take more work than he was willing to put in. And it did feel good to be around friends again, joking and laughing. But instead of making him feel happy like it usually did, it made him realize how many opportunities for the same thing that he'd missed while he'd been in Nestled Hollow.

Eli was exhausted by the time they played their last game and wanted to collapse. But the moment he walked out of the adventure park, the emptiness and loneliness hit him with the fierceness of a storm blowing in.

Chapter Twenty-One

*W*hen Whitney woke up the next morning, her heart felt the pain before her brain caught up enough to remember why. She decided the best course of action to deal with missing Eli would be to throw herself into her work. She wrote three articles, edited four more, interviewed someone about a service project they were doing, called two of her suppliers, worked on the next layout, emailed a couple of advertisers, and texted everyone who was going to help get the leaves and lights ready to remind them to meet at Back Porch Grill at seven. All before Scott and Kara made it in to work after school, and all without thinking about Eli more than a few dozen times.

The informal team meeting she always had with Scott and Kara when they arrived had stopped the momentum she had gained, though, and left her sitting at her desk, her mind wandering again. She touched the letter she'd framed that she had gotten from Mr. Annesley, turning the paper over to her. Every time she was discouraged or overwhelmed, she reread it and a different part would stand out to her. Today, it was the part that said "Be strong. Don't be afraid to go after what you want" that stuck with her.

What exactly did she want? And how could she possibly go after it? Every answer she came up with to those questions scared her. She didn't think she was strong enough to go after any of them. Mr. Annesley had always believed in her, though, long before she ever believed in herself. She trusted him.

A text message lit up her phone, and Whitney picked it up off her desk. It was from Brooke.

I'M BAAAAACK! WHICH MEANS IT'S TIME TO MEET FOR DINNER. I KNOW YOU'VE PROBABLY GOT PREP FOR FALL MARKET. CAN YOU MEET EARLY? LIKE 6:00 AT BACK PORCH GRILL?

Whitney didn't even have to think about it. She needed to get out of her own head and talk about Eli with someone else.

YES, PLEASE! I'LL MEET YOU THERE.

When she arrived at the restaurant, Brooke was already inside, talking with the owner. "We need that booth over there in the corner and out of the way. Pretty please?" She made a show of batting her eyelashes. Cole, the owner, made a show of rolling his eyes, then chuckled and led them to the booth.

"So," Whitney said as she looked at her menu, "how was New York? How was meeting the designer you were going there to see?"

Brooke's words came out in a rush. "It was incredible and he loved my designs and he wants to license two of my dresses to create them and sell them to his distributors and he has a lot of pull in the design community, so this has some potential to go even further."

"What? Brooke, that's so amazing! Wow! That's about the furthest thing from being blacklisted there is. Congratulations!" The whole time Whitney was talking, Brooke was giving her the *hurry up and get to the end of your story* gesture.

"Yep, it's awesome and exciting and all that. Small talk over." She placed her menu at the edge of the table, like she was setting the conversation aside, too. "Now let's get on to talking about you and Eli and why you didn't text me about him once while I was gone."

Whitney looked down as she set her menu on top of Brooke's. "We broke up."

"What?" Brooke exclaimed. "I feel like I can't trust you to make good decisions in my absence."

Whitney chuckled.

"Seriously, though, what happened? I figured the two of you were headed for perennial bliss."

Raising one shoulder in a shrug, Whitney said, "He had a work thing and headed back to Sacramento much earlier than he had planned."

"So that's it? He had to leave, and now it's over?"

It sounded like such a weak excuse when she said it out loud. She wasn't about to relive the emotions she'd had over the past several days, just so that Brooke would understand better, though. "What am I supposed to do? He chose to leave, just like he did last time."

Cole walked over to their table. "You look like a couple of ladies who have figured out exactly what they want."

Whitney let out a single huff of a laugh. Figuring out what she wanted felt like the most unobtainable thing in the world right then. But she did know what she wanted to eat. "I'll have a club sandwich with chips and a giant Cherry Coke. I'll need it for tonight."

"I'll make sure to keep the refills coming."

"And I'll have the chicken pesto panini with soup and a water with lemon. Surprise me on the kind of soup."

He winked, said he'd get it right out to them, gathered up their menus, and walked away.

Brooke put her elbows on the table, her chin resting on her palms, and studied Whitney. After a moment, she said, "Tell me about when your dad died."

Whitney's brow furrowed. "Why?"

"Just tell me."

"He got cancer during my sophomore year." Whitney took a deep breath. "He told me he'd beat it, but he didn't. He died that summer."

"Were you close?"

Whitney nodded. "The closest. As close as my mom and my sister are."

Brooke bit her lip, looking off into the distance, thoughtful. Then she turned back to Whitney. "Who left you next?"

"Left me?" Whitney's confusion turned into an eye roll. "Brooke, we don't—"

"Humor me."

"I know what you're doing."

"Humor me anyway."

Whitney huffed, and then said, "Eli. The first time around."

"That was graduation night, right?" After Whitney's nod, she said, "And you didn't hear from him again until this trip?" Whitney nodded again. "Who's next on your list of people who've left?"

Whitney sighed. There was no use fighting— Brooke was

relentless when it came to getting information out of someone. "My sister, the beginning of my junior year of college. My mom joined her in South Carolina the beginning of my senior year."

"Did they ask you to join them?"

"I still had a year at D.U., and I was dating Ryan, and it was just starting to get serious. Plus, I had my job here at the paper. So no." When Whitney's mom had moved, she'd prayed to know if she should go, and she had gotten the distinct impression that she should stay. She had assumed at the time that it was because of Ryan, but after he left and she was recovering from heartbreak, she had prayed again, and still felt like it was important that she stay.

"What happened with Ryan?"

Whitney looked up and nodded a thank you to Cole as he wordlessly set their drinks in front of them. She pulled the wrapper off her straw and swirled it in her drink. "We got engaged after college. He was an ambitious business analyst, and wanted to be in a big city. So we had planned to live in Denver, and I'd just commute to the paper. Then when we started a family, we'd move here and he'd commute.

"But I guess he had his eyes set outside of Colorado, and didn't bother telling me that he had been secretly applying for jobs in New York and Boston. He got a job offer two months before our wedding date, and left ten days later. He'd asked me to join him, but I hesitated. I'd realized how much this town had become my family when I had none, and everything about moving felt wrong. I begged him to stay in Denver, but he said his career was more important than Denver. He'd love me to join him, but leaving was more important than me, too."

Brooke scoffed and rolled her eyes. "Sounds like you

dodged a bullet there. Goodness, girl. No wonder you've got issues. Next?"

This game was getting old, fast. "Mr. Annesley." Whitney crossed her arms.

"I think he died right before I moved here."

"He'd been my boss since I was sixteen. In many ways, he was my adoptive dad, and his wife was my adoptive mom. He told me I was the closest thing he had to a daughter."

Brooke sucked in a breath. Movement caught Whitney's attention, and she looked over to see that Cole was carrying a tray with their food over to their table, which was good, because she didn't think she could've handled Brooke's response just then, and she knew she definitely couldn't handle her own reaction if she kept thinking about Mr. Annesley.

"A club sandwich with chips for you," Cole said as he set a plate down in front of Whitney. "And a chicken pesto panini for you with a cup of Tuscan vegetable soup." A second later, he placed a second glass of Cherry Coke in front of Whitney. "Figured you might need this."

A laugh escaped, and she wiped an errant tear. "Thanks."

"Anything for a couple of my favorite people." He took a breath and opened his mouth like he wanted to say something more to Whitney, then thought better of it, and just gave her a sympathetic smile. She wouldn't have known what to say to her, either.

Whitney wasn't feeling particularly hungry, but she wasn't feeling particularly like meeting Brooke's eyes, either, and at least eating was something to do. She picked up her sandwich and took a bite.

"Do you wish your dad had died when you were a baby?"

"What?" Whitney nearly choked on her sandwich. She

quickly finished chewing and swallowed. "No! Why would you say that?"

"Do you wish you'd never known your mom or your sister? Do you wish you'd never worked with Mr. Annesley? Or that Ryan had never been in your life?"

"Of course not!"

Brooke put her elbows on the table, arms crossed, and leaned forward. "Then why are you running from a relationship now, just because there's a chance he'll leave? All those people you just listed in your life who have left— wouldn't you say they were the most influential people in your life?" Whitney nodded. "When you told me Eli was leaving, you asked 'What am I supposed to do?' You're supposed to *fight*, Whitney. If he is someone worth falling in love with, he's someone worth fighting for. Are you in love with him?"

Whitney looked down at her sandwich and chips, not really seeing them. Her voice came out a whisper. "Yes, I'm in love with him."

Brooke reached across the table and held both of Whitney's hands in hers. "Listen. I know it's scary letting someone in when there's a good chance that you'll open your heart and be hurt. But you won't lose him by being vulnerable. You'll lose him by pushing him away from your heart."

Whitney thought about how well she'd built those walls around her heart. Could she truly take them down and let him in, regardless of what happened after? Could she try to make a relationship with Eli work, even if she could be hurt all over again? Could her heart handle being hurt again?

"They say fortune favors the brave. Be brave, Whitney." Brooke picked up her sandwich and took a bite.

Whitney pulled out her phone and looked at the response her mom had sent after she'd said to set up the interview. *For real? You want me to set it up? But you love Nestled Hollow! Is this Whitney talking, or fear?*

Brooke, her mom, Mr. Annesley—they were all saying the same thing.

Whitney picked up her sandwich, too, and the two of them ate in silence as everything ran through her mind. What, exactly, did she want from Eli? What was she willing to give? Could she really be that brave?

She studied her friend across the table. Brooke was one of the most fearless people she knew— she had just flown to a party on one side of the country to meet a designer, then flew to the other side of the country to present her creations to a designer he'd recommended her to, and it paid off in spades.

But of course, Whitney wasn't Brooke.

But she was Whitney. And she *was* brave— she was brave enough to run an entire newspaper without a mentor. She was brave when she chose to live in a town half a country away from her only family. She could be brave when it came to relationships, too. She didn't know if Eli was interested in trying to make it work, but she decided she was determined to do everything she could.

"You're a good friend, Brooke."

"I know. *That's* why you love me— not just because I never stay in one place long enough to be pushed away."

Whitney laughed a hearty laugh that apparently she'd really needed by how good it felt. Then she said, "Thank you."

The talking at the front of the restaurant suddenly got louder, and Whitney turned to see Gloria, Donald, Christy, Mike, Sherry, Evia, and the Stone family. "Must be seven." Whitney took one more quick bite, then finished off the first Coke and took a few gulps of the second. "I need to head into the other room to work on decorations. Are you doing anything?"

Brooke picked up her napkin and dabbed at her mouth. "Nope, and as usual, I'm up for anything. So whatever you've got planned, count me in."

Whitney grinned as Cole walked up to their table with a paper cup and lid in his hand. "Dinner's on the house tonight, ladies. Have fun with the Fall Market preparations."

"You're the best, Cole," Brooke said.

It was hard to tell through Cole's scruff, but Whitney was fairly sure he blushed. He glanced toward the doors. "It looks like you've got a good twenty people heading in there already and more on the street coming this way. I'm betting you'll need this," he said as he finished pouring her second Coke into the paper cup and handed it to her.

Whitney gave him a heartfelt thank you, and headed into his side room.

The space was large, open, had good lighting, and was filled with people ready to help. Whitney demonstrated how she wanted various lengths of string tying leaves to the strands of lights. Then she assigned some people to start stretching out the one hundred strands from wall to wall, and some to deliver boxes of leaves, strings, and scissors to everyone who sat spread out on the floor among the strands of lights.

Happy chatter filled the room as everyone worked. Now that everything was laid out, she was able to see how truly monumental the job was going to be. She hoped that happy chatter stayed strong through to the end, no matter how long it took.

She sat down at one of the strands of lights and started working. As she looked around at the crowd that had now swelled to at least thirty-five, she realized that she was ready to stop surrounding herself with people that she kept at a distance. No matter how painful it was going to be to tear down those walls around her heart, she was ready to start. She had been praying again to know if she should move, and right now, watching everyone, she got that same distinct impression that it was important to stay. She sent up a little thank-you prayer to God for giving her His answer. She pulled out her phone and sent a text to her mom.

WILL YOU CANCEL THAT INTERVIEW FOR ME? I'M SO SORRY, MOM. I'LL CALL AND TELL YOU THE FULL STORY LATER. THE SHORT VERSION: YOU WERE RIGHT; IT WAS FEAR TALKING. BUT I'VE DECIDED TO BE BRAVE, WHETHER IT ENDS IN HEARTBREAK OR NOT.

Chapter Twenty-Two

*A*s Eli and Ben waved goodbye to their friends at the adventure park, Ben walked with Eli to his car.

"We'll have to do that again soon," Ben said. "It's been too long."

"It was fun." Eli hadn't realized how badly he'd needed it until he was there. "I'm glad you talked me into it."

Ben studied him for a moment, and then said, "You're always the life of the party. Even on days like today, when you feel like dirt, you're the one with the jokes, making everyone laugh."

Eli cocked his head to the side, not sure where this was going.

"But you don't let people in." Ben studied him for a moment. "Why did you let me in?"

"Maybe because you saw me at my lowest and didn't judge me for it. Plus, we make a pretty good team."

Ben's grin lit up under the street lamp. "You're a brilliant businessman, Eli. You really killed it today at Smithfield."

"Thanks. You too. We've got a good thing going here."

Ben looked at his watch. "We finished the day at TeamUp, and it's now after midnight and no longer Friday, so I figure bringing up Whitney is free game now." Ben cleared his throat. "So, Eli Treanor, as someone with the aforementioned qualities of 'brilliant businessman,' are you honestly telling me that you can't think of a single way to keep both TeamUp and Whitney?"

Eli tossed and turned all night, Ben's question continually running over and over in his mind, keeping him from being able to fall asleep. He must've fallen asleep at some point, though, because he woke to the sound of his phone ringing.

"Hello?" Eli's voice came out groggy and scratchy.

"That was a crap thing you did, leaving your mom in charge of the store."

"Dad?" Eli sat up. "Why? What happened?" He'd talked with his mom about it for quite a while before he left, and she'd seemed fine with it. She'd been helping his dad with the store for the past thirty-two years, after all. She had done every part of every aspect of running the store, even if it wasn't something she did regularly. And Grace was an excellent shift manager, so he'd really thought it would be fine for him to be away while his dad finished recovering.

"Nothing *happened*. But she shouldn't have to have that extra stress on her. She isn't used to running the entire store by herself."

"Did Mom say she was stressed about it?" Maybe it was his cloudy brain from a terrible night and still trying to emerge from the fog of sleep at... what time was it? He pulled the phone away from his face long enough to look. 7:03. But he was having troubles understanding what his father was trying to tell him.

"No, because your mother's tough. The point is, I asked *you* to run the store while I recovered."

Ahh. So that was the real reason his dad was upset. "I was under the impression that you weren't particularly happy with the way I was running the store."

He grunted. "You actually did some good things."

His dad had practically whispered the words, and they were jumbled together so much they sounded like a single word. "What?"

"I said you ran the store well," his dad said, this time in a more frustrated voice.

A smile started to form on Eli's lips. "It really does physically pain you to give me a compliment, doesn't it?"

"And comments like that make me want to take them back." He let out a huff, then a few slow breaths, like he was trying to be calm again. "Anyway, that wasn't what I was calling you about."

"Oh?" Eli got out of bed and walked to his bathroom, curious to see how awful he looked after such a bad night. His eyes were puffy, he definitely needed a shave, and his hair was so far past the kind of messy that could be considered a style it had moved to the kind of messy that bordered on *man raised by wolves who then stuck his finger in a light socket.*

"I was calling to talk about Whitney."

Eli froze, then walked back into his room and sat on the edge of his bed.

"It was tough making this call, because, well, matters of the heart are more your mom's territory, not mine, but this is important. You there? You listening?"

"I'm listening, Dad."

"Well, you know we like Whitney. Truth is, we're rather fond of you, too. And we think you and Whitney are perfect for each other. Always have been."

Eli was so stunned that those words just came out of his dad's mouth that he couldn't form words.

"Why haven't you ever gotten married? I mean, you're thirty years old, son."

After yesterday and the night he had, he was finally being truthful to himself. He might as well be truthful to his dad, too. "Because no one else has ever been Whitney."

"Good. So you feel it, too."

"Dad, the issue has never been whether or not Whitney is perfect for me. I've always known she is. The issue is me not being perfect for her."

Another grunt from his dad. Then the line went silent for a moment before he said, "Tell me, why do you think she's never gotten married either?"

"I..." He realized he didn't know.

"Did you ever stop to think that maybe she hasn't for the same reason as you? That she's not married because no one else is Eli?"

Did he dare even hope that was her reason?

"Now I know I tend to focus on pushing you to reach your potential and getting frustrated when you don't do as well as I know you can. And I haven't been great at saying things like 'I love you' or telling you when you do something that makes me proud. But son, I do, and I want what's best for you. Your mom and I both do. And we can't imagine anything being better for you than Whitney."

His dad paused, and when Eli didn't say anything, he added in his usual gruff voice, "Now you get your rear end back here and run the store like you said you would until I recover. I don't want your mom to have the stress of running the store by herself. You hear me?"

For the first time in his life, Eli did. "I love you, Dad."

After a long pause, his dad said in a low voice, "I love you, son."

Eli didn't move a muscle for several long moments after he hung up the phone. He had understood something while talking to his dad that he hadn't ever understood before. An emotion from his dad that had always been buried under his gruffness and inability to show emotions to Eli. Maybe even something that been there all along.

His dad really did love him. Maybe he was even a little proud of Eli.

He kept thinking through what his dad had said over and over as he took a shower, shaved, and got ready for the day. Somewhere amid all the thinking, a realization hit him. He had been letting his dad's inability to say he loved him make him feel unlovable. But even worse than that, he had been letting that be his excuse to back away from Whitney all along.

Because if it was his dad's fault and not his that he felt unworthy of Whitney, then it wasn't his fault that he had made the poor decision not to call her over and over and over again for the past twelve years. He hadn't ever truly believed it, but he had always heard that forgiving someone wasn't something you did for the person who wronged you— it was actually something you did for yourself to help you move on. Maybe they were right and it would help him.

Because maybe part of learning to forgive his dad also meant letting go of the crutch that blaming his dad had become.

And maybe learning to forgive also meant learning to forgive the stupid, younger Eli who left Nestled Hollow in the first place. Because if he could forgive Younger Eli, then maybe he could move forward, with nothing holding him back, and do everything in his power to get Whitney to forgive him.

Terrible night or not, Eli was suddenly feeling like maybe he could take a much needed turn to get his life back on the track he'd wanted it to be on all along.

Chapter Twenty-Three

A couple dozen people showed up before the sun to help Whitney set up, and she was eternally grateful for the help. Sam from facilities had been stretching the lights across Main Street since 5:00 a.m. so he wouldn't be in everyone's way with his equipment, and he was nearly finished.

She split the volunteers into six groups, and had each group set up one archway and wind leaf garlands through their arch. Mrs. Davenport stopped by to help—she had a maple tree with the most beautifully colored leaves, and she had snipped enough small branches for them to wind through all six archways, making Whitney feel like she was truly stepping through a canopy of trees to enter Fall Market. Each group also laid out the bales of hay to block any cars from being able to enter Main Street, making it a pedestrian mall for the day.

Then they positioned the fire pits, loaded them up with wood and tinder, and placed the logs around them for seating, all while the Main Street businesses and the local and county vendors set up their shops. And then they all took on the massive job of spreading all the boxes of leaves that she and Eli had gathered across both blocks of Main Street.

When they were finished, Whitney stood at the archway near Treanor's and admired their work. It was even more incredible than she had imagined it would be. Between the leaves hanging from the light strands and looking like they were falling from the sky, the outdoor feel from the fire pits and leaves on the ground, the businesses setting up their booths and spreading out their fall-colored wares, and the mountains nestled so close in the background, the place looked like a fall wonderland.

Whitney turned to see Ed and Linda Keetch step through the archway behind her. Linda laid her hand on Whitney's arm and said, "I've lived here since I was a little girl, and I have never seen this street look more beautiful. I knew if I paired you and Eli up for the job that magic would happen."

Whitney turned and looked at Linda. The older woman's eyes were sparkling, like maybe she was referring to more than just the decorations when she'd said *magic*. "I just wish Eli was here to see it."

Linda looked at Ed, then reached out and entwined her fingers in his before turning back to Whitney. "The thing about love is, most people are only willing to let someone in to a portion of their heart. If you let someone in to your whole heart, that's when a little bit of heaven comes down and you get to live your life basking in it."

"Thank you, Linda. Truly."

The thought of opening her entire heart was terrifying. But for the first time in a very long time, she was ready. Whitney pulled out her phone and took pictures of how amazing everything looked before the streets got crowded. Eli deserved to see how everything turned out, regardless of what happened between the two of them. She just wished the pictures could do it justice.

∼

Once they opened Fall Market to the public, people swarmed in. The joint effort of everyone in the Main Street Business Alliance had accomplished miracles, because there were more people shopping than Whitney had ever seen before. Their makeshift parking lot in the field was overflowing. People were heading into shops with their scavenger hunt papers in hand and eager looks on their faces. She stepped into the Gazette and grabbed her nice camera to take pictures for the paper. With this many people, all the businesses would definitely go into winter doing well enough financially that even if they didn't get much snow, they'd still survive.

Throughout the day, she, Scott, and Kara took turns manning the Gazette's booth and handing out free Fall Market editions of the paper. When she wasn't at the paper, she checked in with all the booths, made sure everyone had what they needed, and made sure the stage was set up for the band. She worked with the band— a group of five Nestled Hollow High School kids— to get their equipment set up, and even raced across town in her car with Kylie, one of the band members, to grab an amp they'd forgotten.

As she went from task to task, she wondered if she could ever possibly work things out with Eli. How could she show him that she wasn't afraid of letting him in anymore? That she was ready to give up all her fears and doubts and worries so that they could be together?

She pulled out her phone once more and looked at the

screen. She had texted him several times throughout the day, asking if they could talk, but she hadn't gotten a response yet.

The Back Porch Grill, Keetch's, Joey's Pizza and Subs, and some of the food vendors were just starting to serve dinner and the sun was starting to light the sky with brilliant colors. She gathered members of her volunteer team, and they went from fire pit to fire pit, lighting the fires. The band took their places on to the stage that sat on the bridge right in the very center of Main Street and tuned their instruments. The sun dipped behind the mountains, and the temperature dropped noticeably. People not already sitting at the outdoor tables chatting and eating dinner started flocking to the fires, warming their hands and sitting on the logs, chatting.

Everyone turned their attention to the stage at the center when Ed Keetch tapped on the microphone, and said, "Will everyone please join me in welcoming our very own *Flight of the Mountain Ducks!*"

Everyone cheered, then the hundred strands of lights strung between the buildings from one end of Main Street to the other lit up, and the cheers changed to expressions of awe, Whitney's included. She had imagined this exact moment dozens of times, and it still blew her away. Having the fall leaves hanging from the lights had definitely been the right choice. She used her work camera to capture at least part of the magic on film.

The teens were playing covers of songs from big hair bands in the eighties and nineties, and the crowds were immediately re-energized. Some shopped more, some ate dinner, and quite a few gathered around the campfires or on the road in front of the band.

As the band played the first few chords of *Livin' on a Prayer* by Bon Jovi, a dozen little kids ran out to the empty space in front of the band and started dancing.

"Can I take the camera?" Kara asked.

Whitney jerked in surprise— she hadn't even seen Kara walk up to her.

"I just want to get a few pictures for the paper. Or do you need it right now?"

Whitney ducked under the strap and handed it to Kara. "It's all yours. Take all the pictures you'd like."

Hanging out here all day and seeing all the things that she and Eli created together tore her insides apart. She had socialized with so many people in the past nearly twelve hours, and now she truly understood that even though she loved every single one of them, all the friendly relationships in the world didn't make up for one really deep, meaningful relationship, where she actually let someone inside the wall she'd worked at reinforcing for so many years. It made her miss Eli even more.

She pulled her phone out one more time, hoping and praying for a missed text or call from him, but there wasn't one. She decided that if he didn't text back by the time Fall Market was over and she finished cleaning up, she was going to go to her apartment, pack a suitcase, drive to the Denver airport, and get on the next flight to Sacramento, no matter how late it was.

The band started playing *Right Here Waiting* by Richard Marx, and Ed Keetch stood up from where he sat on a log next to a campfire, holding a hand out to his wife. Linda took his hand, and he led her to the open area in front of the band and danced with her. Moments later, they were joined by several other couples in love.

Normally, a scene like this would've grabbed her heart and made her feel all warm inside as she watched. For the first time in a very long time, though, she'd been able to actually picture herself as someone who could've been out there, dancing with a man she was in love with. But she'd let fear take that away. She was about to go find somewhere else to be, where she could nurse her broken heart in solitude until the festivities were over, when all one hundred strands of lights above went out.

Alarmed, she took half a dozen steps toward the city building, where the power switch was located, when she realized that although the band's singer had stopped singing, the band kept playing, their soft melody seeming to move along with the creek that ran down the middle of the road. All the happy chatting from the crowds had stopped, and through the lights from the campfires, she could see that all the people on her side of the road were slowly moving toward the sidewalks in front of the buildings, leaving the street empty.

She took a few steps forward, confused, not understanding what was going on when everyone else seemed to.

Then she saw a small light bobbing down the creek. A few seconds later, a second light came into view. Then a handful of others, each light bouncing off the waves of Snowdrift Springs, dancing along its surface. She walked to the nearest pedestrian bridge to get a closer look at what was in the creek. More and more and more lights wove their way down the water. As the first one neared, Whitney's hands flew to her mouth, her breath shallow. It was a swan, folded out of a square of what looked like parchment paper, a votive candle resting on its back. Hundreds and hundreds of swans made their way down Snowdrift Springs, each one sending a flicker of candlelight bouncing off the water.

Her breaths became quick, deep, and ragged as she scanned the area for Eli, praying that the swans were from him. A movement off to the right caught her eye, and Eli stepped from the crowd, wearing a suit, looking stunningly perfect, and striding straight toward her. She'd have run to him if she weren't frozen in shock in the middle of the pedestrian bridge, seeing the man who hadn't left her mind since they'd broken up four days earlier.

Eli's steps quickened and he took the last few strides right up to join her on the bridge. "Whitney," Eli said as he grabbed both of her hands in his.

"Eli," she breathed. "You... This is so beautiful." She looked back at the creek, where more and more swans continued to float down it.

"I love you, Whitney. I've loved you since we were sixteen and first became friends. I loved you when we started dating at eighteen. I've loved you every single day over the past twelve years I've been gone, even when I wasn't willing to admit it. You're all I've ever wanted. I'm sorry it took me so long to figure out how to stop running." He reached out and tucked a curl behind her ear, running his knuckles along her cheek. "Please tell me you'll give me a second chance."

Whitney's breath caught in her throat, emotion rising up and washing over her. She reached up and placed her hand on his cheek, grounding her and steadying her, letting her know that he was the reason why she was supposed to stay in Nestled Hollow. She was supposed to stay here long enough to reconnect with Eli. "I'll move."

A look of surprise crossed Eli's face.

"I'll move to Sacramento to be with you." She would've never guessed that she'd be okay with moving away from Nestled Hollow, but the moment the words left her mouth, she was at peace with it. She knew that being with Eli was more important than anything she'd built here.

"And leave all this?" he said, gesturing at the town and Fall Market and everyone on Main Street, who she now realized were all watching her, some taking pictures and videos with their phones, Kara right in front taking pictures with the paper's camera.

"None of this is worth it if it means being without you."

"You would do that? You'd leave Nestled Hollow for me?" His voice came out choked, full of emotion.

"In a heartbeat."

Eli placed his hands on her face, cradling her head, and bent down and touched his lips to hers in the most heartfelt, sweet kiss Whitney had ever experienced. She closed her eyes and soaked in everything about it. Then she put her arms around his back and pulled him in close, deepening the kiss, to the cheers of the crowds around them. Eli chuckled, his mouth still against hers. "We've got a bit of an audience."

Whitney pulled back, so she could look in his eyes. "Speaking of which, how is it that they all seem to be in on this?"

He smiled that crooked smile that she loved so much. "You left with Kylie, but not before getting that microphone set up, and, well, Ed and Linda Keetch and this entire town had my back. This is a pretty cool town. I haven't given them nearly enough credit. And Whitney?"

She noticed that she'd been staring at his lips, and took her gaze back to his eyes.

"We're not leaving Nestled Hollow."

Confusion filled Whitney. "You love TeamUp. You can't—"

He put a finger to her lips. "And I can't take you away from here." He looked around at all the people watching them with smiles on their faces. "I couldn't deprive this town of the one and only Whitney Brennan."

Even though his words were wildly overstating her importance and made her feel awkward, they also warmed her heart. She liked that Eli saw her as being someone that mattered to people.

"They need you. Besides, a good friend helped me realize that I can have both TeamUp and the woman I love. Ben and I had been looking to grow our business, and it turns out that having a second TeamUp location here is exactly what we need. Nestled Hollow can be a destination training facility. I can run the team building activities down by the lake, and in the lake, and even in the mountains. It'll bring more business to Treanor's and to other town businesses, especially the hotels and the restaurants, and I can be here to help run my parents' business, so they can take some time off now and then to enjoy each other. And then maybe the two of us can take some weekend trips together to Sacramento every month or two. That is, if you'd like me to stay here."

"I'd say, Eli Treanor, that there isn't a single part of me that doesn't think that's the most wonderful idea I've heard in my life."

Eli raised her hand up and kissed her knuckles. "Then you have made me a very happy man." He motioned to someone down the street, and the strings of lights overhead came back to life, and the band started playing again. He looked up at the leaves hanging from them taking it all in. When his eyes met Whitney's again, he said, "We do amazing work, don't we?"

She bumped her shoulder into his. "*We* do amazing work? I seem to remember you skipping out on the 'work' part of our amazing work."

He bumped his shoulder into hers and led her down the

bridge to the street. "I'm going to make up for the twelve years we lost, and I'm going to make up for that, too."

Epilogue

Although the past month had been busy, it had been hands-down the best month of Eli's life. He had made several trips back and forth between Sacramento and Nestled Hollow, moving, hiring and training someone to help out Ben at TeamUp, setting things up with Smithfield, getting things set up in Nestled Hollow, and spending every second he could with Whitney.

He leased some land near the lake with an old cabin that he was having renovated into TeamUp offices, found an apartment to live in, and worked out an agreement with the city to use both the lake and the shore to do some of his training programs. He'd also partnered with his parents' business to use some of the equipment, and partnered with both Home Suite Home and All Nestled Inn for local lodging and all three restaurants and the bakery for catering. It had felt good to be back in town again and working together with other people in town to find a solution that was mutually beneficial for all of them.

When he and Ben got together, they had come up with

team building activities that could be done in the winter, summer, fall, or spring, at the TeamUp grounds, by the lake, or in the mountains, so they could run TeamUp Nestled Hollow year round. They already had a handful of bookings and quite a few more in the works. Everything was finally feeling like it was coming together. And now that he understood his dad a little more, and knew that his gruff way of speaking didn't necessarily mean what Eli had been interpreting it to mean all those years, their relationship had improved. It didn't mean his dad didn't get frustrated all the time and lose his temper with him, though. But Eli understood him in a way he hadn't before.

Eli knew that with a new venue, there would be a lot of activities they'd never run before, and he needed to test them. So he invited everyone in town who would like to participate to come down to the lake to try out some activities. The weather had already turned fairly cold, but here they were, on the Saturday before Thanksgiving, having an unseasonably warm and beautiful day— the warmest one they were going to get before next spring. A good fifty people had shown up to play, and they'd already run through enough spring or fall activities that he knew he'd have some excellent ones to start off the spring season with. They were about to do one that was clearly a summer activity. This was the one he was most nervous about running.

He stepped onto the portable riser he had set up on shore so that he could stand above the crowd and see everything. He switched on the headset microphone that led to the new sound system that TeamUp had purchased.

"This activity is actually going to be in the water. I know it's cold, so I've brought eight wetsuits to take the chill off, just in case you fall in the water. See these team paddle boards over here? We'll have four people to a board. It can get a little tippy and make things tricky to get everyone standing, so you'll have to communicate to make it work.

"Your goal will be to get your team to that red buoy out there and pick up the inflatable drink cooler in the shape of a pink flamingo with a crown on its head that's looped to it. The first team to get the flamingo, and get back to shore with all team members still on board, wins. I need eight volunteers. Who's in?"

A dozen hands shot up, including Whitney's. He knew she'd volunteer— she was much too competitive to turn it down. Which was good, since he'd planned on choosing her whether she raised her hand or not. He picked the eight people, and climbed down from the riser to help them get into the wetsuits, and to make sure each player had a life jacket and an oar.

He zipped Whitney's wet suit the rest of the way up. "Are you excited for this?"

"Thrilled," she said, grabbing his shirt and pulling him closer before planting a kiss on his lips. "Sure you don't want to join me?"

They had been outside for hours, and she still smelled amazing. "Always." He and Whitney had been together every moment that they weren't both working, and he still couldn't get enough of her. He glanced at the riser. "I think I better 'join you' from up there, though."

She grabbed her life jacket and swung it on, and he picked up the oar and handed it to her before she joined the others on the shoreline. Eli split them into two groups, then climbed back onto the riser and switched his mic back on.

"Okay, we've got one group over here with Matt, Liz, Hilarie, and Peter— what do you want your team called?"

"Team Speed!" Matt shouted out.

"So we've got Team Speed over there, and here we've got Sara, James, Reese, and the very lovely Whitney. What do you want your team called?"

The four of them gathered in a huddle, talking in low voices. Then they all turned to face him, and Whitney said, "Our team name is 'The Winners.'"

"You can't—"

"Don't dis our team name," James said. "We worked hard on that."

Eli chuckled. "Okay, and over here, we have 'The Winners.' You're really going to make me keep saying that, aren't you?

"Okay, teams, get your team paddle board in the water and line up by it along the shore. Everyone else— this is a tough challenge, so your job is to cheer them on. Now I expect you to be loud, so they can hear you even when they're clear out there by the buoy. Ready? Set? Go!"

Both teams raced forward. "Oh! It looks like we've got two different tactics for getting on the board. Team Speed has left their board solidly anchored on the shore while they get on, and it looks like that's going fairly well so far. The Winners gave their board a good shove out into the water, and they're all trying to get on it while in the water. Reese has gotten on the board, and is lying on his stomach, right across the middle. Either he's doing it to keep the board steady while everyone else clambers on, or he got that far and just gave up. And if that's the case Reese, I'll just take this moment to ask you, *Is that something a member of The Winners would do?* Now, as you can see, Reese's back shaking from laughter. Unless that's just the strain from holding the board steady, because things aren't going so well for those trying to climb on.

"Meanwhile, the members of Team Speed are all on their

board, but they're having some troubles shoving off the edge. Push a little harder, team! Oh, but not so hard that Hilarie falls off. Okay, now Hilarie is shoving them away from shore and hopping nimbly onto the raft. Nice work, Hilarie! Both teams are all on board and standing, oars in the water, heading toward the Royal Pink Flamingo, and now they're neck and neck!"

The crowd of townspeople surrounding him was now cheering so loudly their voices were going hoarse.

"It looks like Team Speed has pulled into the lead, coming right up to the flamingo, and Liz is leaning out to grab hold of the rope and lift it over the buoy. Better catch up quickly, Whitney, Sara, Reese, and James, or you won't be living up to your team name. Look at this— Peter has grabbed hold of Liz's hand so she can reach out further and oh no! A little too far, Liz. So now that Liz is down in the water, The Winners are going for the flamingo. And it looks like Whitney has it in her hands! And she must have forgotten about the rope and it jerked her back. So both teams have a team member in the water, and now there's a battle for the flamingo! It's impossible to tell from here who is winning. What do you guys think?"

The crowd around him started shouting out "Liz" and "Whitney." Eli crossed his fingers and sent up a little prayer. His whole plan hinged on Whitney's team winning.

"And Whitney just flung the royal pink flamingo onto The Winner's paddle board and instead of getting on board as well, she has opted for holding onto the back and kicking the paddle board forward as the rest of her teammates paddle with all they've got. After a couple of unsuccessful grabs at Whitney, Liz has given up and is now clambering back onto Team Speed's board. They're reaching down and pulling her on board and nice job keeping that board steady, Team Speed!"

Come on, Whitney, Eli silently pleaded as she stayed pushing the board from behind, kicking her feet in the water. *Get back on the board before you reach the shore.* What was he thinking, leaving so much to chance on something so important? *Have faith in her,* he told himself. Whatever team Whitney was on always won.

"Team Speed is paddling like a sea serpent is after them," Eli said into the mic. "It looks like their strategy might be to catch up to The Winners and make a grab for the flamingo. As we're coming into the home stretch, cheer like your team's win depends on it!"

The crowd's cheering intensified, and Eli's heart raced. He couldn't find words to commentate the race as Team Speed got closer and closer to closing the gap, and The Winners were only twenty feet away from the shore. And then fifteen feet. *Get on, Whitney!* he silently pleaded.

Then, ten feet before the shore, she let her feet drift down. She must've been able to touch the bottom of the lake to push off, because she shot into the air, leaping onto the board, landing on her stomach.

"Wow! Did you see that leap? The Winners now have all their teammates on the board, they've got the royal flamingo annnnnnnnd.... Yes! They made it ashore with Team Speed making it to the shore just two seconds behind them. Congratulations, The Winners! Because it would've been really embarrassing to lose, with that being your team name. Give yourselves some high-fives, because you really deserve it!"

The crowd cheered even louder, clapping the members of both teams on the backs and giving high-fives. All eight contestants took off their life jackets, dropping them in the sand, and heaving big breaths while grinning.

When the cheering died down a bit, Eli said, "TeamUp—"

And the crowd responded with "To triumph!" They had learned well throughout their day of challenges.

"Whitney, since you're the one who pulled the flamingo out of the water, why don't you come join me up here, and we'll see what your team won."

Whitney grabbed hold of the flamingo, and walked up the three steps it took to join him on the five foot square platform. She placed it on the railing, and he unzipped the back of the flamingo, revealing a place to keep two or three cans of soda inside.

"Well, Whitney, show us what The Winners have won!"

"We each won a Hundred Grand!" Whitney said, pulling out the four candy bars. Whitney handed the candy bars to Eli, and he tossed them to her teammates.

"Wait," she said, and Eli's heart thumped even harder. "There's something else in here." She pulled out a red velvet heart-shaped ring box, a question on her face as she held it out.

"Aww!" someone in the crowd yelled. "She won your heart!"

"That she did," Eli breathed as he stepped close enough to kiss her. He took the box in one hand and used the other to brush some wet hair off her face. Even soaking wet from lake water, she was the most beautiful woman he'd ever seen.

He dropped to one knee as the crowd collectively gasped. "Whitney," he said, "never in my life have I been as happy as I am whenever I'm with you. Please say you'll marry me, and I'll spend the rest of my life making sure you're just as happy." He opened the ring box, and the sun's rays hit the diamonds, making it brighter and more beautiful than he'd ever seen it.

"And the cheesiest line goes to..." Whitney said, a smile spreading wide, her face beaming.

Eli couldn't help the smile that spread on his face. "Say you'll marry me, and I'll fill your life with cheesy lines until the day I die."

"Promise?"

"I promise."

"Oh, Eli," she said. "Of course the answer is yes! It's been yes for as long as I can remember."

She let him slip the ring onto her finger, and then she pulled him to his feet and kissed him, a fierce love behind her lips, filling him from his head all the way down to his toes. He'd nearly forgotten that they were surrounded by four dozen people until the deafening cheer rose around them. Their kiss turned into smiles. "I love you," Eli said against her lips.

"And I love you," Whitney said. "Forever and ever."

Author's Note

I hope you enjoyed reading Whitney's and Eli's story as much as I enjoyed writing it!

Would you like to read a prequel to the Nestled Hollow Romances books? Joselyn's and Marcus's story, where the ice cream shop first opens, is free when you join my newsletter! You can get it at www.megeaston.com.

Want more Nestled Hollow? Pick up the next book in the seres —*Christmas at the End of Main Street*. This Christmas, Macie and Aaron are teaming up to make everyone believe they're dating each other so they'll quit trying to line them up with others.

May you have many hours of happy reading in your future!

—Meg

READ NEXT: CHRISTMAS AT THE
END OF MAIN STREET

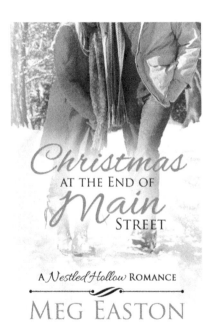

GET THE SERIES

Coming Home to the Top of Main Street
Second Chance on the Corner of Main Street
Christmas at the End of Main Street
More than Friends in the Middle of Main Street
Love Again at the Heart of Main Street
More than Enemies on the Bridge of Main Street

ABOUT MEG EASTON

Meg Easton writes contemporary and inspirational romance. She lives at the foot of a mountain with her name on it (or at least one letter of her name) in Utah. She loves gardening, bike riding, baking, swimming before the sun rises, and spending time with her husband and three kids.

She can be found online at www.megeaston.com, where you can sign up to receive her newsletter and stay up to date with new releases, get exclusive bonus content, and more.

Made in the USA
Las Vegas, NV
19 December 2020

13911396R00115